*A new daytime drama
brought to you by*

Judie Angell

SUDS

BRADBURY PRESS
SCARSDALE, NEW YORK

Special thanks to Donald Jensen, scientist and aviator, for some technical advice—J.A.

Copyright © 1983 by Judie Angell.
All rights reserved. No part of this book may be reproduced or transmitted in any form or by any means, electronic or mechanical, including photocopying, recording or by any information storage and retrieval system, without permission in writing from the Publisher.
Bradbury Press, Inc.
2 Overhill Road, Scarsdale, N.Y. 10583
An affiliate of Macmillan, Inc.
Collier Macmillan Canada, Inc.
Manufactured in the United States of America
10 9 8 7 6 5 4 3
Library of Congress Cataloging in Publication Data
Angell, Judie.
  Suds, a new daytime drama.
  Summary: Grief-stricken after the mid-air collision of her parents' planes leaves her an orphan, Sue Sudley moves to her aunt's small mid-western town where she hopes to become "a real teenager."
  [1. Orphans—Fiction] I. Title.
PZ7.As824Su 1983 [Fic] 82-22732
ISBN 0-02-705570-1

114015

Thank you for this book, R.J.
I had such a wonderful time!
and
A sudsy greeting to D.S.P.,
who can at *least* still feel the sun on his
hands

Cast (*in order of appearance*) . . .

SUE SUDLEY, *poor little rich girl*
Nanny Grossup, *family retainer and Sue's governess*
Paige Stillwater, *Sue's aunt*
Nick Stillwater, *Sue's uncle*
Carson Stillwater, *Sue's six-year-old cousin*
Mooch Deener, *local bus dispatcher and father of Dinah*
Storm Ryder, *the Stillwaters' next door neighbor and former football star*
Dinah Deener, *flunking student and video-games junkie*
Knuckles, *the Ryders' dog*
Arlette Levine, *student and local gossip-gatherer*
Rick, *Dinah's (and others') boyfriend*
Matt Argus, *sports reporter for the school paper*
Bunny Ryder, *Storm's mother*
Larchmont, *the Sudleys' chauffeur*
Benita Deener, *Dinah's mother*
Mr. Coffee (Joe), *English teacher at Palatine High*
Melissa, *changegirl at Leon's Neon*
Marcia/Whitey, *a duck*
Roger Gurney Jr., *senior at Palatine High and editor of the school paper*
Bonnie Finster, *well-endowed cheerleader*
Emily, *veterinarian's receptionist*
Dr. Krass, *veterinarian*
Roger Gurney Sr., *Roger Jr.'s father and editor of the* Palatine P.M.-Daily

Mr. and Mrs. Hegelmeyer, *Charlie's parents*
Charlie Hegelmeyer, *duck owner*
Joanna Coffee, *the English teacher's wife*
Will Ryder, *Storm's father*
Dr. Proctor, *neurologist*
Leon, *owner of Leon's Neon*

EXTRAS: *video-games player, newspaper staffers, football players, ambulance attendant, nurses, doctors, rowdy crowd, man with Chihuahua*

As you remember . . .

We left Sue Sudley in a deep emotional decline, staring at the canopy above her bed at Suddenly, the family mansion, with only old Nanny Grossup in attendance, and nightmares of the ghastly accident haunting her.

That June day that began as a happy celebration and ended so tragically replayed itself over and over in Sue's mind in a catastrophic kaleidoscope:

—Her mother deciding to surprise her father on Sue's fifteenth birthday by flying herself and Sue in the family's Cessna 182 Skylane to his corporate convention on the west coast.

—Her father deciding to surprise Sue and her mother for Sue's fifteenth birthday by flying himself home in his Lear jet.

—The midair collision . . .

—Sue, hanging from her birthday present—a multicolored designer parachute—watching in horror as her parents' plane fragments fall to earth . . .

—The double funeral.

Then, finally—the silence of Suddenly, the soft blue drapes blotting out the harsh July sun, and except for the quiet patience and sympathy of old Nanny Grossup, Sue was all alone.

— * —

From our last episode . . .

"Oh, Nanny, if it weren't for your quiet patience and sympathy, I'd be all alone!"

"Here, Miss Sue, won't you have some cocoa? I've put some marshmallows in it . . ."

Sue lay back against the pillows and stared at the canopy once more.

"Please, Miss Sue? You've hardly had a bite in weeks."

"All right, Nanny, I'll try . . ." But she didn't reach for the cup. She began to count again the number of Yves St. Laurent signatures running around the edge of the canopy.

"Mummy just loved designer things," Sue said aloud without realizing it.

"Yes, she did, Miss Sue. She loved having people's names on all her possessions . . ."

"And mine," Sue said.

"And mine," Nanny sighed.

"I never really cared for that, you know . . ."

"I know, Miss Sue. But you wore everything . . ."

"Oh, yes, it pleased Mummy, so what did it matter? I wanted things to be pleasant for her . . ." She touched her welling eyes with a linen handerchief. "Whom can I please now?"

"You can please yourself now, Miss Sue," Nanny said with a slight tilt of her head. She waited as Sue played idly with the edge of her pillowcase. Finally, she said, "We've talked about the paths you can take . . ."

"Yes," Sue said thoughtfully, "I could stay here at Suddenly with you . . ."

"You could . . ."

"I could sell Suddenly and you and I would take an apartment . . . I'd really hate to sell it to that movie star who asked about it. He wants to re-do the swimming pool in the shape of a barbell."

"You could sell it to those people who want to turn it into a Senior Citizens' summer camp, Miss Sue. Just think of all the people Suddenly can please!"

"I know, I have thought about it . . ."

"Your Uncle Benton offered you a home with his family," Nanny said softly.

"Uncle Benton is Daddy's brother . . . The life I'd have with him would be just like the life I've always known. Besides, I'm not really sure he wants me."

"And then there's your Aunt Paige."

Sue smiled wanly, but Nanny noticed it was still a smile: the first she'd seen since the accident.

"They seem like such lovely people, Miss Sue."

Sue looked over at her night table. Behind the pictures of her mother and father in their matching flying helmets and white scarves was a family portrait of her mother's younger sister, Paige, with her husband, Nick Stillwater, and their little daughter, Carson.

"Mrs. Stillwater said she wanted you with her so badly, Miss Sue," Nanny said. "Remember her last words as she and Mr. Stillwater were getting into their pickup truck after the funeral?"

"Yes . . . she said, 'I want you with us so badly, Sue.' "

"Miss Sue, I hope you won't take offense, now . . ."

"Oh, Nanny, you know you can say whatever you want! Please."

"Mr. and Mrs. Stillwater and little Carson . . . you know they live a very different kind of life in Palatine, Ohio than the one you've been used to here at Suddenly."

"That's exactly what I've been thinking, Nanny."

"No designer clothes and canopies and maids' uniforms . . ."

"Yes, Nanny! I'd have a chance to be like any other teenager. No chauffeur to take me to school, no enormous rooms to rattle around in, no dressing for dinner—"

"You *have* been thinking, Miss Sue," Nanny said with a smile.

"Yes. Yes, I have. I've always wanted to be like real kids, Nanny. A life with Aunt Paige and Uncle Nick and Carson sounds so exciting to me . . . but . . ."

"But what?"

"But I feel guilty thinking about this new life, when Mummy and Daddy—" Her eyes filled again.

"Now, Miss Sue," Nanny said, patting Sue's hand, "you'll always have the memories of your mum and dad. But you have to go on with your own life. And starting fresh—in a new town, a new way of living, with people who love and want you—"

"But—Nanny, do you think another person in the house would be too much for Aunt Paige?"

"Miss Sue, you've never given anyone a lick of trouble in your whole life and I don't think you're about to start now. They'll be lucky to have you! And you'll be lucky, too."

"A real teenager," Sue murmured, almost to herself. "I'll do it, Nanny! I'll sell Suddenly to the Senior Citizens and I'll go live with Aunt Paige and Uncle Nick!" Then the excited expression which had fleetingly lighted up her face faded. "But, Nanny, what about *you*? And what about Larchmont?"

Nanny flushed slightly at the mention of the chauffeur, but Sue didn't notice.

"Don't you worry about Larchmont or me. We'll be fine. I'm sure they'll be able to find some use for our services at the Senior Citizens' camp. And we'll never be out of touch with you!"

"Of course not!" Sue cried.

Nanny clasped her hands together. "You're going to find yourself, Miss Sue," she said with a smile. "You're going to find out who you really are."

"Who I really am . . ." Sue whispered.

And almost before she knew it, Sue was being met at the Palatine bus terminal by the Stillwaters.

— * —

A week before
Labor Day . . .

"Oh, Sue . . ."

"Oh, Aunt Paige . . ."

"Oh, Sue . . ."

"Oh, Uncle Nick . . ."

"Oh, Cousin Sue . . ."

"Oh, Carson . . ."

They all hugged each other.

"Where are your things, honey?" Paige asked. "Surely they're not all on the bus . . ."

"No, Larchmont, our chauffeur, is driving them out in the limo and a U-Haul trailer."

Nick took Sue's arm and began to escort them all out of the bus terminal. He proudly turned to the bus dispatcher, seated at his window, and called to him.

"Hey, Mooch! Here she is! Our little niece! Sue, over there's Mooch Deener!" And he whispered to Sue: "Good customer at the taproom!"

She nodded and smiled at the dispatcher. "Hello, Mr. Deener," she called.

"Hello, there," Mooch answered. "Welcome to Palatine, Sue!"

"Thank you."

"Have a daughter about your age," Mooch said. "Guess you'll meet her . . ."

Sue nodded and smiled again as Nick opened the door of the terminal.

"Why didn't you drive out with your chauffeur, Sue," Paige asked, "instead of taking the bus?"

"I felt like taking a long bus trip," Sue explained. "I wanted to . . . just look at the scenery. And besides, there wasn't room in the car or trailer. I'd have to sit on the propeller."

"The *propeller?*"

"I wanted a memento of . . . Mummy and Daddy. You could put it on the bar, Uncle Nick . . ."

"Yeah, that'd be different," he allowed.

"How come you didn't fly, Cousin Sue?" Carson piped. "It's a lot faster than the bus!"

"Hush, Carson!" Paige said, and turning to Sue, added, "she's only six."

"That's all right, Aunt Paige. I understand."

"Come on, folks," Nick said. "Here's the old baby!"

They piled into the Stillwaters' station wagon and Nick took the long way home in order to acquaint Sue with their little town.

"There's the high school, Sue," he said, pointing. "Pretty modern, don't you think? Got a campus and everything!"

"Yes . . . It's very nice, Uncle Nick . . ."

"Don't cry, Cousin Sue," Carson said, touching her arm. "School doesn't start for two more weeks!"

"Look, Sue, there's the bar! Put on a whole new front since you last saw it. 'Course you were only about four and wouldn't remember, but it's real imitation marble with real imitation mounds of grass out front! Nice, huh?"

Sue looked up at the carved wooden sign over Nick's establishment: *Stillwater's Taproom*.

"It's lovely, Uncle Nick," Sue sighed.

"Yeah, you gotta see the inside."

"Can't wait . . ."

"Next block, Sue," Paige said, turning around in the front seat. "We're almost there."

Nick pulled into their driveway behind his pickup truck, just as a group of young people were arriving at the house next door.

"What's going on at the Ryders'?" Carson squeaked. "Who are all those kids?"

"They're Storm's friends, Carson," Paige answered softly.

"Oh."

"Storm?" Sue asked.

"That's his nickname," Nick said, climbing out of the car. "Star of the ninth grade football team. Kids called him 'Storm' because of the way he stormed down that field! Boy, he was great! Could've been something . . ."

Sue got out of the car and looked at the boys and girls being admitted to the house.

"Could have been?" she asked.

"The Ryders are lovely people," Paige said quickly. "Storm's mother and I are good friends. Storm's just your age, Sue—fifteen . . ."

"Isn't he still a football star?" Sue asked. She smiled as Carson tried to drag her one suitcase out of the back of the car.

"Not any more," Nick said. He took the bag from Carson.

"Let's not go into that now, Nick," Paige said. "Please?

Sue's just gotten here and she'll hear all the neighborhood news soon enough—"

"Storm had an accident," Carson announced. "A bad one."

"Now, Carson, please, let's go into the house—"

They walked toward the front door.

"It's all right, Aunt Paige, really," Sue said. "You don't have to hide anything from me."

"It was a moped accident," Paige said. "Storm is very popular, you can see how his friends all support him—"

"What happened?" Sue persisted.

"He went out of control."

"And?"

"Now, Sue, really, we can talk about Storm some other—"

"Aunt Paige, I don't need to be protected. I've been protected all my life. I want to be here with you and Uncle Nick and Carson and . . . contribute something and be a real person."

"All right, Sue . . ." Paige smiled at her and they stepped into the Stillwaters' small living room. "Well, it *was* awful. Storm careened through the wall of the revivalists' tent out on Route I-42. Knocked over all of the pews on the right hand side and ended up under the weight of the crashing pulpit."

"Terrible!"

"Mahogany."

"How awful," Sue said, shaking her head. "But he did survive . . ."

"Oh, yes. But he's lost the use of his legs."

"Poor Storm!"

"But that's all he's lost, Sue," Paige said. "He's a lovely

boy! So smart and friendly . . . I'm so anxious to have you meet him. You do have something in common, each of you having suffered a tragedy this summer and—"

"Of course—" Sue interrupted quickly. "I would . . . like to meet him . . . I'm anxious to meet everyone, Aunt Paige, but . . . I just got here and well, I need a bit of time . . . I know you understand."

*

Storm Ryder looked around at the group of his friends who were seated on the floor at his feet.

"It sure was nice of you all to come," he said and smiled at them.

"Well, we all care for you, Storm," Dinah Deener said sincerely, touching his knee.

One of the girls on the floor began to struggle with a large brown dog.

"Get down, Knuckles!" Storm cried. *"Down!"*

"It's all right, Storm, he's not hurting me, really," the girl said.

"I can see him chewing your skirt, Arlette . . ." Storm tried to grab the dog's collar.

"Well, it's an old skirt . . ."

"Sit, Knuckles!" Storm bellowed and the dog grunted and sat. "I'm sorry, Arlette. He's changed a lot since . . . since my accident. I think he's gotten very protective."

Arlette reached out a tentative hand and patted the dog's head. He growled and she pulled away quickly.

"Say, this sure is a great wheelchair you all chipped in to buy me," Storm said to the group.

Dinah's boyfriend, Rick, said, "Yeah, we knew you'd like it. The day-glo orange really jumps out at you!"

"It's the only part of me that will ever jump again . . ."

"Oh, Storm, don't!" one of the girls cried. "You're going to do just fine!" and a boy said, "Yeah. Football may be out, but you're still president of this year's tenth grade!"

Arlette said, "You know, Storm, all of us have taken days. One of us is going to push you back and forth to school all the time!"

"You don't have to do that, Arlette," Storm protested.

"No, Storm, we *want* to, don't we, kids? We want to show you nothing has changed as far as our friendship is concerned."

"Boy. I just don't know what to say."

"You don't have to say anything, Storm," Matt Argus said. "That's why we're here today, to get you all prepped for school and to let you know we're all behind you."

"Literally," Rick added.

"I appreciate it, really I do," Storm said. "But you guys won't have to push me. The school board's voted me a special bus and Mrs. Coffee's going to be driving it."

"The English teacher's wife?" Matt asked.

"Uh huh. Mr. Coffee got her the job."

"Hey, Storm," Rick said with a grin, "how do you like the little alligator on the backrest of the wheelchair?"

"Real neat," Storm said, reaching to touch it. As he moved, Knuckles gave another low growl.

"Down, Knuckles . . ."

Knuckles' teeth clamped down on Rick's shoe.

"Knuckles!" Storm yelled.

"It's okay, Storm, I've got a high pain threshhold," Rick said as Mrs. Ryder appeared in the doorway.

"Mom, I think you'd better do something with Knuckles," Storm said. "He's bothering everybody."

Mrs. Ryder shook her head. "I just don't know what's come over this dog, Storm," she said, tugging Knuckles by his collar.

"He misses our time together," Storm said, looking down at the dog. "All the runs I used to take him for . . ."

But his mother was determined to lighten the mood.

"There are two big boxes of pepperoni pizza out in the kitchen," she said, smiling at the kids. "Who'd like some?"

They all dove for the pizza except for Dinah, who broke out from pepperoni.

*

The last to leave, Dinah and Rick sat down together on the Ryder stoop.

"Don't you have to be home?" Rick asked.

"I don't care. I want to sit for a minute. With you," Dinah answered.

Rick shrugged, "Okay," he said.

"I think Storm was glad to see us," Dinah said, leaning against Rick's shoulder.

Rick stretched, forcing her away. "Yeah. Ahhhh. . . ." He flexed his arm muscles. "Yeah, I think he was. Poor guy."

"He'll be all right. He's still got his brains. He's still smart. The accident didn't change that."

"Come on, Dinah," Rick said, frowning at her. "Don't

start with that smart business. It really makes me mad. You're smart enough."

"Oh, no, I'm not, Rick. I have to repeat three of my ninth grade courses . . ."

"So what? That doesn't mean you're not smart."

"Oh, no? What else does it mean?"

"It could mean you didn't work hard enough. You were always out. With me. Right?"

"Not always . . ."

Rick stood up. "Don't start that either, Dinah. I'm not taking out anybody else except you."

"That's not what Arlette says."

"Arlette talks too much. You can't believe anything anybody says who talks that much."

"She says you're always drooling after Bonnie Finster."

"I don't drool."

"And not only Bonnie, either—"

"Hey, look!" Rick was staring at the house next door.

"What?"

"Look! Look at the size of that limousine pulling into the driveway!" Rick cried.

"Wow!" Dinah breathed. "And look at that beat-up U-Haul attached to it!"

"Yeah!"

"I didn't know the Stillwaters had a limousine . . ."

"Me neither. Guess he must do okay with that bar of his . . ."

"Look, the chauffeur's unloading stuff!" Dinah stood up, too, and they both moved closer to the Stillwater property.

"Look-a those trunks!" Rick whispered.

"Leather, they look like."

"Yeah, with brass trim. Boy, is that a bed canopy?"

"Look at that beautiful set of matched luggage!"

"And the skis!"

"Somebody's moving in there, I'll bet," Dinah decided.

"Well, that's weird . . ." Rick said, wrinkling his nose.

"What?"

"Chauffeur's just carrying in a propeller."

*

"Larchmont!" Sue flung herself at the chauffeur who was obviously pleased but embarrassed. He gingerly patted her back. "I didn't expect you until tomorrow!"

"Well . . . I wanted you to have your things, Miss Sue," Larchmont said. "I drove straight through the night."

"Oh, Larchmont . . ."

"That was lovely of you, Larchmont," Paige said. "Wasn't it, Nick?"

"Oh," Sue cried, "I'm sorry. I was just so glad to see you. You have met Aunt Paige, haven't you, Larchmont? Mummy's baby sister? And her husband, my Uncle Nick—"

"Mr. and Mrs. Stillwater," Larchmont said. Paige thought he bowed, but she wasn't sure.

". . . And this is little Carson," Sue finished.

"Hi, I saw a real chauffeur once on TV," Carson said, grinning.

"Miss Carson." Larchmont nodded.

"Well!" Paige said, moving about her kitchen. "We were just about to have some coffee. Won't you join us, Larchmont?"

"Oh, no, thank you, Mrs. Stillwater." Larchmont stood stiffly in the middle of the floor for a moment before turning to Sue. "I—I'd best be going, Miss Sue," he said.

"No! Larchmont, you just got here! Is there a new job you have to get to? What are you going to do?"

"Well, I—I—"

"You don't have any place to go, do you, Larchmont?" Sue said.

"I—well—not really, Miss Sue . . . Suddenly's been sold . . . And you know, Nanny's been asked to stay on and help organize the Senior Citizens' camp. They're hoping to open next summer and she'll have a year to work on it—"

"Oh, she'll be wonderful!" Sue cried.

"Yes, she will. But—here I am, suddenly without Suddenly."

"Oh, Larchmont, couldn't they use you at the camp, too?"

"Perhaps when it opens, Miss Sue, but for now—"

"I think I have an idea," Paige said, pouring Nick's third cup of coffee. "Nick, haven't you been worried about that rowdy crowd who's been coming into the bar at night lately?"

"Uh, well—"

"Nick's been worried about this rowdy crowd who's been coming into the bar at night lately," Paige explained to Sue and Larchmont. "Wouldn't it be wonderful, Nick, if you had a *bouncer?*" She cocked her head toward Larchmont.

"A what?" Nick asked.

"I beg your pardon," Larchmont said.

Sue explained, "A bouncer is someone who works for

nightclubs and bars and things and takes care of people like a rowdy crowd—"

"Yes, Miss Sue, I know what a bouncer is, but I hardly think—"

"Oh, but Nick needs someone, don't you, Nick?" Paige cried.

"Well, " Nick said, "they're not *that* rowdy . . ."

"You said they were rowdy!" Paige said. "And you have that little office in the back . . . with a daybed in it . . ." She prodded Nick with her finger. "*I'd* certainly feel safer if you had someone with you at night, Nick."

"Well, maybe you're right," Nick said slowly.

Larchmont cleared his throat. "Please, Mrs. Stillwater, Mr. Stillwater, I do thank you for thinking of employing me, but I don't believe this is quite the position I—"

"Oh, but Larchmont," Sue interrupted. "You have no place to live now, no job—and if you stayed here in Palatine, we'd be near each other. Please think about it, Larchmont—"

Larchmont hesitated. "But, a *bouncer,* Miss Sue?"

"You'd make a wonderfully dignified bouncer, Larchmont," Sue said firmly.

"Yes, I think so, too," Paige added. "A sort of combination maitre-d' and bodyguard."

"Real class," Nick said, smiling.

"And you'd be near Sue!" Paige finished.

Larchmont coughed again. "Well, I—I would like to— Why, I've known Miss Sue all her life."

"*Please,* Larchmont," Sue begged.

"Tell you what," Nick said. "Why don't we go on down there? I've got to open the bar anyway. I'll show you the place and you see what you think. How 'bout it, Larchmont?"

The chauffeur smiled at Sue who was looking pleadingly at him. "Very well," he said, nodding. "Let's have a look."

*

Mooch Deener arrived home at the same time as his daughter, Dinah. She was alone, but Mooch had seen her boyfriend, Rick, duck behind a fence as he drove by.

"Hello, Daddy . . ." Dinah said, as she climbed the porch steps.

"I saw him, Dinah. Don't pretend you've been by yourself all this time."

Dinah sighed and opened the front door.

"Home, Benita!" Mooch called as they walked in. "Your daughter, too, for a change!"

Benita Deener came into the living room carrying a flower arrangement which she placed on a corner table.

"Hi, dear," she said, She kissed Mooch. "And hi, dear." She kissed Dinah.

"She's been with that boy again," Mooch told his wife. "Tried to hide him while they were walking home."

"Well, I wouldn't have to do that if you'd just leave me alone about him," Dinah complained.

"I just hope you don't see him when school starts, Dinah," Benita told her. "Your grades were terrible last spring!"

Dinah decided to change the subject.

"We—I was over at Storm Ryder's," she said. "All the kids were there. He feels so depressed—you know. So we wanted to cheer him up. And guess what we saw afterwards?"

"What?" her mother asked.

"Next door at the Stillwaters'—a *chauffeur* in a *limo* was unpacking a whole bunch of *gorgeous* stuff!"

"A chauffeur, huh?" Mooch said. "The girl came in by bus. I met her today at the terminal. Nick and Paige were picking her up."

"What girl?" Dinah asked.

"I told you," her mother said. "Mrs. Stillwater's niece."

"What niece?"

"Dinah, you never pay attention. The niece who's parents were killed in that awful double plane crash. Her mother came from here. She went east years ago. A chauffeur, did you say? Well, I heard Paige's sister married very well . . . There was certainly a large obit in the *P.M.-Daily.*"

"Didn't *you* marry very well, Benita?" Mooch asked playfully.

"Of course, I did, Mooch. You know what I mean. I only hope Dinah marries well, too!"

"Not if the only one she ever hangs around with is that bum Rick," Mooch mumbled.

"Daddy, don't start," Dinah said firmly. "I love Rick and I want to see him as much as I can."

"Yeah, well, it's not mutual, Dinah," her father growled at her. "I see him coming into the bus terminal all the time, hanging around, waiting to see the pretty girls who get off the buses—"

"Stop it, Daddy!"

"Well, it's true . . ."

"It is not! Rick only sees me! And I'm not staying here to listen to this!"

"Where are you going?" Benita asked, as Dinah opened the front door.

"Down to Leon's Neon, that's where!"

"Video games again! Dinah, why can't you read a book or something?" her mother asked.

"I'm going to Leon's! Pac-Man loves me, even if you don't!" She hesitated inside the doorframe. "I need some money . . ." she said.

"She needs some money!" Mooch echoed. "First she insults us and then she asks for money!"

"Isn't that what kids do?" his wife asked.

"She needs some money!" Mooch repeated, throwing his hands in the air.

"You insulted me, too, Daddy," Dinah whined. "You insulted my taste in men. And besides, pretty soon you'll be going on the night shift down at the terminal and then you won't see me so much any more because I'll be at school when you're home and think how guilty you'll feel because you won't be spending any time with your child!"

"Did you hear that?" Mooch cried to Benita. "Now she's trying to make me feel *guilty* so I'll give her what she wants!"

"Isn't that what kids do?" his wife asked.

Mooch turned to Dinah. "Two dollars," he grumbled.

"Only two—"

"Out!" Mooch bellowed.

"I'm going, I'm going," Dinah said, pocketing the bills. "But that's only eight games. Or six games and a soda."

"Well, you have to be home for dinner," her mother said. "Honestly, Dinah, I simply don't understand the attraction those bleeping and buzzing and blinking games hold for you!"

"They clear my head!" Dinah shouted and slammed the door.

*

While Dinah was running toward Leon's Neon to clear her head and Nick was taking Larchmont to the bar, Paige and Sue sat sipping coffee in the Stillwaters' kitchen.

"That was a wonderful idea Aunt Paige," Sue was saying, "getting Larchmont that job at Uncle Nick's bar. What a nice thing to do!"

"Well, honey, I did it for us, too. I really would feel better if Nick had someone down there with him. I worry about that rowdy crowd who's been coming into the bar at night lately and I know he does, too, even if he doesn't say so."

"I just hope Larchmont agrees to stay."

"My, you have a lot of suitcases, Sue," Paige said, glancing over at the ceiling-high pile in the hall.

Sue sighed. "I know . . ." she said.

"Well, don't worry, we'll get it all unpacked eventually. Oh, Sue, I'm so glad you're here, I've got so many plans . . ." She reached over for her copy of the *Palatine P.M.-Daily* that had been delivered that afternoon. "There are just so many things going on in Palatine . . ." She began to turn pages. "Hmmm . . ." she said, suddenly engrossed.

"What is it, Aunt Paige?" Sue asked.

"What? Oh, I just ran across the Police Blotter, dear . . ."

"Pardon?"

"They print the police reports every week. I always find it so interesting . . ." Paige went on reading.

"Is there a lot of crime in Palatine?" Sue asked.

"Well, see?" Paige said, holding up the paper. "It takes up the whole page. Listen to this . . . 'On Wednesday, an anonymous caller reported a dog having convulsions on Bony Knoll Road. Dog Warden Murphy responded.' "

Sue said, "Mmmm . . ."

" 'Thursday, eleven A.M.: Main Street resident reported seeing suspicious person corner of Main and Richman . . .' " Paige continued.

"Why does he think the person was suspicious?" Sue asked.

"It doesn't say. But listen to this—also on Thursday: 'Two P.M.: Appleby resident reported stolen motorcycle!' "

"You mean you think the suspicious person on the corner of Main and Richman in the morning stole the motorcycle on Appleby in the afternoon?" Sue asked.

Paige tightened her lips. "You never know," she said. "That's why the Police Blotter is so interesting. Oh, listen to this: 'Police received report of couple fighting at Blue Ridge Road residence at 11:03 P.M. Friday.' I'm sure that's the Millers again! Last time he threw a shoe at her in their back yard and it broke the next door neighbors' window! I know it was the Millers, but the paper never says! That's what makes it fun!"

"Has Nick reported the rowdy crowd who's been coming into the bar at night lately?" Sue asked.

"Yes, he did, once. I was so excited to see us in the paper!"

"And what happened?" Sue asked. "Did they arrest anyone?"

"Well . . ." Paige said sheepishly, "we do have a fine police force here in Palatine—both the men are so nice—but sometimes it takes them a while to get where they're supposed to be and they kind of missed the rowdy crowd."

"Oh."

"But with Larchmont there, I'm sure things will be better. Oh, Sue, there's going to be a potluck supper at the firehouse on Sunday! That'll be fun, you'll meet just everyone! And there's a variety show over at the Little League building—all the coaches are doing a cancan—and there's the usual Bingo at the church—well, maybe you don't like Bingo—"

"Aunt Paige—"

"Would you be interested in auditioning for a community theatre production of *Hello, Dolly*? Or how about—"

"Aunt Paige—"

"Oh, I see the Veterans of Foreign Wars are having a parade . . ."

"Aunt Paige—"

"But what are the kids your age doing? Let's see here." Paige ran her finger up and down the columns of the pages as Sue fidgeted in her chair.

"There are just lovely things to do, Sue. On Labor Day there's a picnic down at the beach that the Rotary Club runs and—"

"Aunt Paige, really—I've only just arrived—" Sue said weakly.

"Well, of course, dear, I know. I'm just so excited

about your being here and getting to know people and the town—*I* know, Sue! There's a picture here on page seven of the zoo's polar bear and her brand new cub! Isn't it cute? Honey, tomorrow, why don't we all go down to the zoo and see it?"

"The zoo? Great . . ." Sue said as her eyes crossed.

*

"Well, Larchmont," Nick said, gazing proudly around Stillwater's Taproom, "this is it. What do you think?"

Larchmont pulled back his shoulders and cleared his throat. "Well—"

"Look at the fish over the bar. Stuffed. It's a sailfish. I caught it myself two years ago in Florida. Isn't she a beauty?"

"Well—"

"And the plants over each booth? See the way the leaves drip down a little? They're plastic, but you can't tell in the candlelight, see the candles on the table? In real old fashioned candleholders? Got 'em at an auction. Nice, huh?"

"Well—"

"And look. Here's the piece-de-resis-*tahnce*." He went over and tapped the bar itself. "Look at this. Brand new. Real wood. Real. I polish it all the time. This is the last thing I added, my latest addition. You know those western movies where they slide a drink right down the bar from one end to another? You could do that with mine. Smooth, like glass. Beautiful, isn't it?"

"I—"

"Next year, if things go well, I'm going to get a piano player."

"But—"

"I know, I need a piano, too, but all that's for next year. That'll be class!" Nick beamed.

"A piano," Larchmont said and nodded.

"Let me show you the back room," Nick said. It was a small paneled office with a desk, a chair and a daybed. "We could fix it up, you know, make it more homey for you . . ."

Larchmont coughed. "Mr. Stillwater, I really—I'm not sure I'm the kind of man you need for this establishment—"

Nick put both his hands on Larchmont's shoulders. "Larchmont . . . you're *just* the kind of man I need for this establishment."

Larchmont smiled a pained smile. "Well," he said, "I could give it a try, sir . . ."

"Good," Nick said. "Good. Why don't you try the bed out right now? You've been driving all night, working all day . . . I know the feeling. You take yourself a nice nap right now, while I get ready for the cocktail hour."

When Larchmont had settled in gratefully, Nick went out to begin the ritual he loved: polishing the bar. He was spraying on the Pledge, smoothing with his rag and smiling as a customer came in and sat down on one of the stools.

"Polishing again, eh, Nick? You must love that brand new bar of yours."

Nick didn't look up, but grinned down at the gleaming wood.

"See that?" he said. "So shiny I can see my face in it."

The customer nodded to himself and Nick finally lifted his head.

"Oh, hey, it's you, Mr. Coffee. Nice to see you."

"Nice to see you, too, Nick. Give me a double scotch. Neat."

"Drinking in the afternoon, eh? Guess you must be thinking about school starting soon."

Joe Coffee smiled wearily. He'd been teaching English at Palatine High School for nine years and had twice been passed over for head-of-department.

"No, I'm really looking forward to it, Nick," he said. "It's the book. I got my second rejection slip today . . ."

"That novel of yours? Ah, I'm sorry, Mr. Coffee. But I'll bet there's a publisher somewhere who'll be happy to get it. You're a good writer, Mr. Coffee. I remember that story you had in the *P.M.-Daily* last spring, all about Storm Ryder's accident and how the whole school loved him and everything . . ."

"I don't know, Nick . . . It's different with the book. There's something wrong with the plot. It's dull."

"About small town living, isn't it?" Nick asked.

"Yes . . . it's about living in a small town."

"Small town living," Nick mumbled. "That's what I said."

"The trouble is," Joe Coffee sighed, "nothing ever happens in a town like this . . ."

— ✱ —

Friday,
the first week of school . . .

"Have you *heard?* Have you heard the news about Mr. Coffee?" Arlette called as the kids began to file into the building.

"Yes, you told us, Arlette," Dinah Deener said, brushing past her. "You told us." She took Rick's arm and walked quickly into the school.

"Did I tell *you?*" Arlette asked, touching Sue's sleeve. "Who *are* you?"

Sue looked at her shyly. "My name is Sue Sudley. I'm new here. I live with my aunt and uncle, the Stillwaters . . ."

"Oh! Sure!" Arlette cried. "Next door to the Ryders. Have you met Storm yet? Poor Storm!"

"Well, no, I haven't. Not yet . . ."

They began to walk down the hall.

"Oh, well, how do you like Palatine, are you happy here, where did you move from and how come and have *you* heard the news about Mr. Coffee?"

Sue blinked. "I do and I am, from the east, because I lost my parents, and you mean Mr. Coffee my English teacher?"

Arlette nodded. "I'm awfully sorry about your parents. Yes, the English teacher. Boy, is he cute! And now he's available, too!"

"Available?"

"Yes! See, Mr. Coffee's wife Joanna, she's the bus driver who was supposed to drive Storm to school? You know, in a special bus because of his accident?"

Sue nodded.

"Well, the bus didn't show up on Wednesday, the first day, and Mr. Coffee told everybody his wife was sick and Storm didn't make it to school, but she didn't show up yesterday, either, and that's when the news broke."

"News?"

"Yes! That Joanna Coffee wasn't really sick at all, but she ran off, guess who with?"

"I can't imagine," Sue replied.

"Leon!"

"Leon?"

"Of course! Haven't you been to Leon's Neon?"

"Leon's Neon?"

"You know, the video games center where all the kids hang out. You mean you haven't been to *Leon's Neon?*"

"Well, no, but I haven't been socializing much yet—"

"I'll take you there at lunch. When's your lunch?"

"Fourth period."

"I knew it. Mine, too. I'll meet you here. Oh, did I tell you my name? It's Arlette Levine."

"Oh, but—" Sue began. She wasn't sure she was up to Leon's Neon but she didn't want to offend Arlette, who was the first person of her own age she'd spoken to since she arrived, except for the few kids she'd asked for directions to class.

"See you soon, Sue, I've got to sop up some Social Studies!" Arlette called as she dashed off.

Sue looked after her for a moment and then she thought of her English teacher. Poor man, she thought. Poor Mr. Coffee.

*

"Look at it! Just look at it, isn't it *gorgeous?*" Arlette was holding Sue by the arm and pointing to an enormous sign over two tiny wooden doors. The sign—shimmering, flowing, weaving, in blue, pink, chartreuse, turquoise, green and black letters, proclaimed the establishment to be LEON'S NEON.

"Leon was so cool," Arlette was saying, as Sue shaded her eyes from the glare. "That sign just grabs you, doesn't it?"

Sue said, "It—"

"Come on, let's go in," Arlette said, tugging at her.

"Arlette, I'm not sure I—"

"You'll love it. And you'll meet all the kids!" She pulled on the brass handle of one of the doors and they stepped inside.

The colors, if anything, were brighter indoors. There were games everywhere—games lined up against the walls, games in the middle of the floor, games glittering and flashing, beeping, zinging, growling, exploding. Sue's lips parted; she could feel her pupils dilate.

"Listen, Arlette—"

"Fantastic, huh? Now look, I'm going to tell you who everyone is so you'll know when I introduce you, okay? First of all, that girl over there chewing gum, the one with the little apron, that's Melissa, she's the changegirl. You need to know her for when you want to play the games and to find out who's been in and out and everything. Over there is Bonnie Finster, she's a cheerleader and a real snob about it, isn't she *built,* and over there at the Jungle Pinball, that's Matt Argus, he got all A's last spring semester but everyone knows he stole the answer keys to all the exams out of the supply room first, and—"

The lights as well as Arlette began to get to Sue and she staggered slightly, steadying herself against Space Pinball.

"Oooh, and see the girl in the real tight jeans? No, the other one," Arlette was saying. "That's Dinah Deener, and see the guy she's with? Rick, her boyfriend. Only does he cheat on her! He puts the make on every girl in school. I tried to tell her, but she's so dumb, she doesn't even listen. . ."

Sue wasn't even listening.

*

"Rick, can I have a quarter?"

"I gave you a quarter, Dinah."

"I know, but I used it. Please, Rick? One more?"

As Rick turned away, he spotted Arlette and Sue near the front door of Leon's Neon, and experienced a rush of ambivalent feelings. One person to avoid at all costs was Arlette, but she happened to be with a female person he'd noticed at school and had never met. How could there be a female person at school he'd never met?

"Here, Dinah," he said, reaching into his pocket.

"Rick! Honey! A half-a-dollar?"

Rick shrugged. "Live, kid," he said, and waited until Dinah was happily flipping the flippers of her pinball machine. Then he sauntered over toward Arlette and Sue.

"Hi-i, Arlette," he said in his smoothest voice.

"Hel-lo, Rick," Arlette smoothed back.

"I don't think I've met your friend here. Say, are you okay, honey?"

Sue blinked twice.

"I'm fine," she said. "Really."

"This is Rick, Sue," Arlette said. "Rick, this is Sue Sudley, she's living at the Stillwaters'."

Rick's own inner pinball machine lit up his brain and rang bonus bells. The limousine, the leather luggage, the . . . chauffeur . . . and here was the owner of them all. And not even bad looking!

"Well, *hi,* Sue!" he said and showed her all his white teeth.

Sue said, "Hello."

"I'm Dinah," Dinah said, materializing out of nowhere and taking Rick's arm.

Rick made a face that Dinah missed. "Did you use up that half-a-buck already?" he said.

"No, but I want to save the last quarter for Pac-Man and I have to wait for Bonnie to finish playing." She said all this with her eyes on Sue.

Sue looked at Arlette and then at Rick and when no one introduced her, she nodded politely to Dinah, and said, "Hi, my name is Sue Sudley. I'm—"

"—living at the Stillwaters'," Arlette and Rick said together.

"Yes. Paige and Nick are my aunt and uncle."

"Permanently?" Dinah asked, and this time she was looking at Rick.

"Well, yes," Sue answered, bobbing her head to get into Dinah's line of vision. "It's—"

"Let's go, Rick, it's almost time for fifth period," Dinah said and dragged him toward the door.

"—nice to meet you all," Sue finished.

*

That afternoon Sue tried to concentrate on what Mr. Coffee was saying in her English class, but she kept thinking of what Arlette had told her about his wife running off with the famous Leon. She was wondering who was running Leon's Neon now, when the bell clanged, cutting across her thoughts. Absently she rose and gathered her books, then she realized that Mr. Coffee was calling her name. When she looked up, he was beckoning her over to his desk.

The class filed out behind her as she took the hand Mr. Coffee was extending.

"Miss Sudley," he said warmly.

"Mr. Coffee." She smiled.

"I just wanted to welcome you personally to Palatine High and to my class in particular," he said.

"Thank you. That's very kind."

"I want you to know, too, how touched I was by your essay on *How I Spent My Summer Vacation*."

She looked down. She felt a little awkward because he was still gripping her hand.

"It was most sensitively written," he said.

"Thank you again."

He let go of her hand and motioned her to the chair next to his desk.

"The part about sifting through the plane wreckage—how awful that must have been for you."

Sue looked at her lap. "Yes, it was," she whispered.

"I can imagine. And that almost dreamlike sequence where you notice the colors of the parachute above you as you drift, while below are the gray and black charred remnants of—"

"Excuse me, Mr. Coffee—" Sue choked.

"Forgive me, please. I didn't mean to upset you. I was

deeply moved by the courage it took for you to write this essay and of course, your . . . passion."

"I appreciate that Mr. Coffee," Sue said, thinking that he, too, knew loss. "I thought I could get through this a little better if I could write about it . . . but I'm finding that speaking about it still—"

"I understand. That's a lovely sweater you're wearing, Miss Sudley," Mr. Coffee said next and Sue thought how sensitive he was to change the subject when he felt her pain. She'd never had a teacher speak to her as if she were a real person instead of a little schoolgirl.

"Thank you, " she said for the third or fourth time.

"Yes, it's a lovely shade of black. Deep . . ." he leaned back in his chair. "And what an interesting monogram on it—your initials, I presume."

"Yes. Susan Oglethorpe Sudley. S.O.S."

"Lovely."

This time Sue smiled her thanks.

"Well, I don't want to keep you." He rose and extended his hand again. "It's a pleasure to meet you and to have you in class."

"My pleasure," Sue said. She pulled her hand free and went off to Study Hall. Poor Mr. Coffee, she thought.

*

Paige was unpacking the third trunkful of Sue's sweaters. She'd had Larchmont bring up two old bureaus from the basement in addition to the large one already in the room, but she realized with a sigh that some of Sue's things would have to remain in their trunks against the wall. Carson would be trotting home any minute and she wanted to make a further dent in the unpacking when she heard her doorbell chime. Quickly she hurried downstairs to find her nextdoor neighbor, Mrs. Ryder, standing on the stoop with a small bouquet of flowers.

"Hello, Bunny," Paige said as she opened the door. "Come in. What lovely flowers!"

Bunny Ryder stepped into the living room.

"Thanks, Paige. I brought these for your niece . . ."

"Sue."

"Sue, yes. I feel awful about not having come over before to welcome her."

"Not at all," Paige said. "Here, let me put these in water for her and you come right into the kitchen and have some coffee with me. Carson's due momentarily and I know Sue will be right behind her."

They squeezed into the breakfast nook in the kitchen while the coffee was perking.

"I would have come sooner, Paige," Mrs. Ryder said, "but I've been spending just about every waking minute with Storm . . ."

"Oh, is there anything wrong?"

"Nothing physical. At least . . . nothing *further* physical, except now that school's begun again, he's just . . . so . . . depressed."

"I should have thought being with his friends at school every day would cheer him up," Paige said.

"I'm sure it would, except he hasn't gone to school."

"Not gone?"

"Well, he was to have a special bus. You know, to pick him up and bring him home every day . . . The school board arranged it."

"Yes?"

"Well, Joanna Coffee was to have been the bus driver."

"Oh. I see."

"Yes, and now she's gone."

"She certainly is that."

"Storm's school friends all wanted to come and collect him every day, but Storm was absolutely adamant about not accepting that kind of help from his friends."

"Storm's always been so proud," Paige said, pouring their coffee.

"Exactly. It's his pride. He hasn't been out of the house for days and days. I finally decided it would be all right to leave him for a bit so I slipped out to say hello to your niece. Or, at least, extend our family's welcome. How is she?"

"Well, she's all right . . . She will be, anyway. Right now she says she just wants to stick close to home, settle in, you know—feel her way about . . . Naturally, the accident is very much with her . . ."

"Of course. Poor thing. Perhaps she and Storm might be good for each other, having endured recent trage-dies."

"That's just what I told her," Paige said. "I'm sure they'll meet soon."

"If only I could get Storm to go to school!"

"Can't they find another bus driver?"

Bunny Ryder sighed. "They've looked and looked. Or so they tell me."

"Hmmm . . ." Paige said, resting her chin on her palm. "I just might have the perfect solution!"

*

"Hello? Stillwater's Taproom, Nick Stillwater, here."

"Nick? It's Paige."

"Hi, honey."

"Listen, I've got Bunny Ryder here with me and she tells me they're looking for someone to drive Storm's special bus to school."

"I can't, Paige, this is a busy time and —"

"Not you, Nick! A chauffeur. A *real* chauffeur!"

"Ohhh! A *real* chauffeur!"

"Don't you think Larchmont would be perfect? Then he'd have a job during the day and he could help you out at night! You know, when that rowdy crowd who's been coming into the bar lately shows up—"

"Well, sure, honey. Sounds like a good idea. I'll mention it to Larchmont when he wakes up."

*

Sue and Paige walked into Sue's bedroom in time to grab Carson before her Doctor Scholls' ripped the hem of Sue's beige cashmere skirt.

"I hope you don't mind that I've been trying on your things, Cousin Sue," Carson piped. "They're so pretty!"

"Not at all, sweetheart," Sue said, touching Carson's cheek. "They're made to be worn by someone who loves them." She smiled at Paige as Carson bounced out. "I really love my room, Aunt Paige," she said.

"I'm glad, dear. But it is a lot smaller than the one you had at Suddenly . . ." Paige looked at the clothes and boxes still strewn around the room. "I suppose you had the space there for all these things . . . We've hardly made a dent in this unpacking since you've arrived!"

"Oh, I don't need all this stuff," Sue told her. "I brought it because I didn't know what else to do with it, now that Suddenly's being sold. This room is just the right size!" She reached for a pile of sweaters Carson had tossed on the floor. "And I'm glad I'm here," she added. "Suddenly could never be the same without Mummy and Daddy . . ."

Paige took the sweaters from Sue and put them down on the bed. Then she reached over and hugged her niece tightly.

"It's going to be all right, Sue," she said tenderly. "I know how you feel, but everything's going to work out, you'll see. All the memories won't be so painful once you feel that you're home here. That you belong. What worries me a little is that it's going to be very different for you in Palatine. Nick and I don't live like you did at Suddenly. I remember that house, though I only visited a few times . . . And of course, for the funeral . . ."

"I'm going to be fine, Aunt Paige. I've always wanted to live on a real street with real people and do real things . . . It's just . . . I wish the circumstances had been different, of course . . ."

"Of course, we both do. But for me it's almost like having my baby sister back again. You know," she said, sitting down beside Sue on the bed, "it's amazing how much you resemble your mother. And the two of us talking cosily here in a bedroom together, it's just the way Frances and I used to when we were teenagers."

"Mother didn't talk much about Palatine," Sue said.

"No, I'm sure she didn't. She was so anxious to get away. She left home when she was just seventeen. Going to be a big Broadway star, she said . . ." Paige smiled. "She had so many big dreams . . ."

"I guess I didn't know that side of her . . ."

"Well, her dreams pretty much came true. She didn't get to be a Broadway star, but she—"

"She got to be an important executive secretary," Sue finished proudly.

"Yes, and then she married the important executive. President of the corporation. She left Palatine far behind . . ."

"But now *I'm* here."

"Yes. Now you're here. I hope our life is enough for you."

"Aunt Paige, I feel as if I'm an empty glass jar, waiting to be filled up by experience. Suddenly was like a dreamworld. It was never real. I hardly ever played with other kids, and when I did, Larchmont drove me there and waited around and then took me home. It made my friends nervous and I was hardly ever asked back. And Mummy or Daddy always seemed to screen everyone, and they picked my clothes and—"

"What is it?"

"I shouldn't talk that way," Sue said. "They loved me very much and I loved them, and now they're—"

"Oh, Sue—"

"I do miss them terribly, Aunt Paige. Only there's so much I know I haven't seen. It's so confusing . . ."

"Of course it is, dear. I understand. But you've got to push yourself a little, too, you know. Did you see the flowers Bunny Ryder brought for you? I know you'll be crazy about her son, Storm . . . I can't believe you two haven't met yet—"

"The flowers are lovely, Aunt Paige. And I am beginning to meet some people . . . I guess what I'm doing now is like going to the movies. Watching how the people act on the screen. Learning to settle in . . ."

Paige leaned back and smiled. "Oh, you're a watcher,

are you? You look things over before you plunge in?" She shook her head and her smile widened. "Well, you're not like your mother there! She never even checked to see if there was water in the pool before she dove!"

"I can't imagine Mummy like that."

"Frances changed when she got married. And I don't think it was for the worse, either. We kept in touch. And when Carson was born—"

Carson stuck her head through the door. "You call me?" she asked.

"Carson, it's not polite to listen at doors," her mother said.

"I wasn't listening. I was taking a nap on the rug in the hall."

"When Carson was born," Sue went on, "I remember . . . Mummy and Daddy sent her a pony."

"They did? They did?" Carson squealed. "They sent me a pony? Where is it?"

Paige sighed. "Carson you were an infant. We kept it for three days inside the chicken-wire fence around the vegetable garden. It broke out, ate all the Ryders' prize tulips, and ran off. The police found it trying to kick down the door of the bowling alley."

Carson wailed "I want my pony!" until her mother stood up and sent her off to take a bath.

Paige went to the bureau and put the sweaters she'd folded into a drawer. "Sue, I'm not sure your canopy will fit on the Castro convertible there . . ."

"Oh, that's all right," Sue said. "I never thought of putting it up. The canopy's just kind of a souvenir. It's the only thing I looked at all summer . . ."

"Well, sure, we can stand it up over there in the corner . . . My, Sue, I wonder if we'll *ever* get you un-packed." Paige began folding more sweaters.

"Oh, Aunt Paige, please pick out the ones you like and take them! And then maybe we could have a garage sale for the rest, or something . . ."

"Some will just stay in the trunks, I guess" Paige said absently. "We'll have to move the trunks out, though, if you want to keep the propeller in here . . ." She tapped a blade.

But Sue was staring straight ahead.

"Sue?" Paige said.

"Oh. Sorry . . ."

"Honey, what is it?"

"Nothing . . . Nothing, really. I was just thinking about Mr. Coffee . . ."

"Oh. Poor Joe!"

"He talked to me today about an essay I wrote for him about the accident and Suddenly last summer . . . He was very nice. He talked to me almost as if I were a real writer, not just a student . . . Do you know what I mean?"

"I think so," Paige answered. "I hear he's a good teacher. He's certainly a nice man. That Joanna! And *Leon,* of all the sleazy people! Oh, Sue, that reminds me. I talked to Nick about asking Larchmont to drive Storm's special bus now that Joanna's gone. Isn't that a good idea?"

"A lovely idea," Sue said. "Is he going to do it?"

"I don't know yet . . . He was napping. He naps a lot, doesn't he, Sue?"

Sue smiled. "Well, he doesn't have many diverting interests right now, I guess. He does love to drive and sleep, sleep and drive . . . Maybe he has jet lag from his long trip here."

"But that was three weeks ago . . ." Paige said. She studied Sue while absently toying with the edge of the propeller in the middle of the floor. Poor baby, Paige thought. Such a big adjustment . . . She looked down at the propeller. Hmmmm, Paige said to herself, it's looking awfully dull . . . And those charred spots . . . Well, I think I just might have another wonderful idea!

— ✳ —

Ten days later . . .

Arlette had taken Sue under her wing. She'd decided that Sue needed to be brought out into the world and she, Arlette, would be the bringer. For days she trailed her, following her after class, meeting her at the start and end of school and at lunch. Sue's faint protests were ignored.

"The school paper's a wonderful activity for you, Sue," Arlette was saying as she and Sue left the Science Lab. "It'll give you an outlet for your creativity and you'll be working with absolutely the best minds in the school. I'm on the staff myself."

"Oh, really? What's your job?" Sue asked.

"Publicity. I'm very good at it."

"Oh, I'm sure," Sue said.

"I think you should join. Why not think about it?"

Sue bit her lip. The school paper. She had worked on the paper at her last school when she was a freshman and had found it rewarding. Perhaps it would be easier to be with people now if she had a job to do . . .

"I will think about it, Arlette. I might like to do that . . ."

"Oh, you will, I guarantee it. And speaking of the school paper, here comes our advisor walking down the hall. Oh, he's just so cute I can't *stand* it!"

"Mr. Coffee?" Sue saw him coming toward them.

"Joe-Joe Coffee. Adorable, and now available for action. He's the reason I joined the paper. Hi, Mr. Coffee!" she called.

"Sue. Miss Sudley. How are you?" Mr. Coffee held out his hand and Sue shook it.

"Just fine, thank you . . ."

"Mr. Coffee, I loved the way you did *The Ancient Mariner* today," Arlette gurgled. "I mean, the way you stood on your desk and flapped your arms to show how the albatross—"

"Miss Sudley, there's something I've been meaning to discuss with you. Do you have a moment? My, that's a lovely sweater. An even nicer shade of black. Deeper . . ."

"Mr. Coffee, I've been trying to talk Sue into joining the newspaper staff and she just might—"

"Right in here, Miss Sudley . . . the teachers' lounge," Mr. Coffee said, opening the door he was standing near. "Why don't we talk for a minute . . ."

As Sue found herself being ushered into the teachers' lounge, she glanced over her shoulder at Arlette who was saying brightly, "I knew he'd want to talk you into it, Sue! It was such a good idea, see you next period—" as the door closed in her face.

Sue smiled up at Mr. Coffee. "I don't think I need much talking," she said. "I believe I'd enjoy working on the paper—"

"I'm so glad to hear it," Mr. Coffee said sincerely. "I was going to suggest it to you myself as soon as you've had some time to become settled, and well, you know, adjusted . . . more or less. However, there was something else I had in mind."

"Oh?"

"Have you met a young lady in our English class by the name of Miss Deener?"

A neon light flashed in Sue's mind. "I think so," she said. "I think I have. What is her first name again?"

"Dinah."

"Dinah. Yes. She was with a boy named—"

"Rick. Bad business. Dinah needs a good influence. She could do better if she'd get down to work, but she spends all her time with that boy doing everything but studying. She needs a good friend. Someone with . . . sensitivity. Someone who could help her with her composition work—"

"Oh, that sounds wonderful!" Sue cried. "I'd really love to work with her! Is that what you meant? That I could work with Dinah and help bring out her true creativity and help her express herself on paper the way she can't in other ways—"

"Well, actually, what she really needs is someone to explain that between the words in the composition there should be spaces."

"Oh. Basic help, you mean."

"Very basic."

"Well, sure, I'd like that—"

"And then later on, of course, your special talents, your creative abilities, will be able to play a bigger part."

"It sounds fine, Mr. Coffee," Sue said, smiling.

"And of course, I'd be there to help you organize your lessons."

"Of course."

"Well, then, it's settled. I'll talk to Dinah about it. I'm sure she'll be as pleased as I am about this arrangement."

"Good," Sue said as she took the hand he extended.

*

The door of the taproom opened but Nick did not look up. He continued swishing his chamois cloth back and forth across his bar with large strokes, stopping only now and then to peer at his reflection in the wood and smile.

"Hi, Uncle Nick . . ."

"Hi, there."

"It's me, Uncle Nick—Sue!" Sue bent over the bar so he could see *her* reflection in it.

"Oh, Sue, hello. School out already?"

Sue climbed up on a barstool. "Yes . . . I thought I'd stop in and say hello on my way home."

"Good!" Nick said as he polished. "What can I get you?"

"Oh, just a diet 7-Up." Sue looked around. "The place is looking prettier every day, Uncle Nick."

"Yeah." He grinned. "Like the new stools? They came yesterday. Absolutely authentic imitation goatskin."

Sue ran her fingers over the side of her stool. "Mmmm," she said absently. "Feels like goat . . ."

"How's everything going, Sue?" Nick stopped polishing to ask so Sue knew he was really concerned.

"Well, fine, really, Uncle Nick," she said. "Everyone has been so nice and kind . . . This is just the sort of life I've always dreamed about living. It's only that sometimes I wake up in the morning and I don't know where I am. Everything's so different."

"It just takes time, honey," Nick said and resumed polishing.

"Mr. Coffee suggested today that I take on an English

tutoring assignment. A girl named Dinah Deener needs help."

"Oh, yeah, Mooch Deener's kid. Heard she was having some problems . . ."

"Oh, yes, she is. We have to begin with things like capitals and periods at the ends of sentences."

"No, I meant other problems. Mooch's been in here complaining about some boy she's been hanging out with that he and Benita don't like at all."

"Hmmm . . . Yes, Mr. Coffee mentioned him, too. I think I met him the first week of school at Leon's Neon. He was with Dinah there and Arlette introduced us. Well, Mr. Coffee seems to think it'll work out . . ."

"Mr. Coffee, yeah. Good customer. How about another 7-Up. On the house this time."

"Okay, Uncle Nick, thanks."

There was a pounding at the door—a thudding sound near the threshold as if someone were kicking at the wood.

Nick raced around the end of the bar. "It's open, it's open!" he yelled. "Don't kick it, it's new!" He yanked the door open as quickly as he could.

"Hey, Larchmont!" he cried.

The chauffeur was holding something in both arms, but neither Sue nor Nick could make out what it was because it was completely wrapped in giant towels.

"Come in, come in," Nick said, opening the door wider.

Sue slid off her barstool. "What is it, Larchmont? What have you got there?"

Larchmont didn't answer, but tentatively pulled back some towel edge. An orange beak poked out.

"What's *that?*" Nick cried.

"Quack," the beak said.

"Huh?"

"Quack," the beak repeated.

Larchmont tenderly drew the towels back further. "It's a duck, sir," he said. "It's a duck, Miss Sue."

"Ohhh," Sue cried, reaching for it. "Is it hurt?"

"I don't think so, Miss Sue. However, I nearly ran over it some moments ago. I had just dropped off the Ryder boy at his home and was driving slowly down that little alley—Do you know the one I mean? Near the launderette? Well, this poor thing—" he looked down and jiggled the duck in its bunting—"just waddled right out in the path of the bus. I'm sure I didn't hit it, Miss Sue, because I didn't feel anything, but when I got out, it was just squatting there in the street not moving and I wasn't sure."

"Quack," the duck announced.

"Fortunately, I had some old towels. I always keep some old towels, you never know when they might come in handy. And I just wrapped him up and came here straightaway. Frankly, I—I didn't know where else to take him."

"Maybe he belongs to someone," Nick offered. "Does he have a collar? Tags?"

"Maybe it's a she," Sue said.

"No, sir, no collar, no tags," Larchmont said. "I can't imagine who'd let a nice duck like this go wandering off down the street by itself. I simply couldn't take a chance on someone else hitting it."

"Of course you couldn't, Larchmont," Sue said. "Let's put it down and see if it can walk."

"Here?" Nick asked with a pained expression. But

Larchmont had begun to remove the towels and he set the duck down on the floor.

"Oh, it's one of those big beautiful white ones!" Sue exclaimed.

"Quack," the duck said appreciatively.

"It looks all right to me," Sue said.

The duck turned its head from side to side, studying the bar.

"Would you like to keep it, Mr. Stillwater?" Larchmont asked.

"Well, Larchmont . . ." Nick bit his upper lip.

"Wouldn't Carson be thrilled!" Sue cried.

"Well, Sue, I don't—"

"Probably we should put an ad in the paper about it, though . . . You know, 'Found: Duck,' and then we could describe it. That way at least we'd be trying to find its real home."

Nick nodded. "Sure. I guess we could do that. Meantime we could take it home, keep it fenced in . . . Yeah, Carson sure would love it, all right . . ."

"Quack," the duck agreed.

"Then maybe Thanksgiving, instead of turkey, we could—"

"Uncle Nick!"

"Sorry, Sue, okay . . . It's just, boy, with orange sauce . . ."

"Uncle *Nick!*"

"Okay, okay . . ."

The duck waddled over to the corner and squatted.

"Say, Sue, why don't you take it home *now?*" Nick said. "Before it—you know, before it—does anything. I just waxed."

"I think it's all right, Mr. Stillwater," Larchmont said.

"It's just tired. Here, why don't I put a towel under it and let it squat there for a while . . ."

Sue said, "I'll finish my 7-Up and then I'll take it right home. Larchmont, won't you have one with me?"

"Well, I'd be delighted, Miss Sue. And then I'll be most happy to drive you to your door," the chauffeur said.

"Oh, no, I wouldn't hear of it. Besides, isn't it time for your nap?"

"I'll take you home first, Miss Sue . . ."

"No, please, Larchmont. No more chauffeuring for me. I'm on my own now and I'm certainly capable of carrying a duck! Now, let's enjoy our sodas."

"Quack," the duck offered and moved to another part of the towel.

"Ahhh, I knew it!" Nick grumbled.

"It's all right, Uncle Nick, it's on the towel," Sue said.

"Have you acquainted yourself with the Ryder boy, Miss Sue?" Larchmont asked as he sipped his 7-Up.

Sue shook her head. "No, not yet, Larchmont. Aunt Paige has been awfully anxious for me to meet him, but, well . . . we haven't been introduced yet . . . I think I've seen him, though. Do you like driving him, Larchmont?"

"Oh, yes, Miss Sue, he's a very nice boy. Very nice. Such a pity about that accident. I understand he was quite a football player."

"Quack," the duck cheered. Nick frowned.

*

Rick sauntered down the main street, poking his head toward every store window that interested him. A display of leather aviator jackets impressed him most and he spent a few minutes picturing himself in a brown one with twenty-two zippered pockets.

"Cool," he muttered aloud and continued walking.

He glanced casually through the window of Stillwater's Taproom, then stopped in his tracks and looked harder. Yeah, he thought. That's her, having a drink with some old guy. My kinda woman.

He stared at Sue and Larchmont until Sue got off her stool and walked over to a corner of the room out of his sight. When she stood up, it looked to him as if she were cradling something in her arms. Something large. He watched her turn and say goodbye to Nick and Larchmont, who hurried to open the door for her.

Rick took a few steps backward quickly, so it would look to Sue as if he happened to be passing the bar just as she was coming out. It worked perfectly: he almost knocked her down.

"Gee, I'm sorry," he said. "Guess I was too close to the door. Hey, aren't you Sue Sudley, the Stillwaters' niece? We met at Leon's. I'm Rick."

Sue struggled to get a better hold on the duck in its towel. "Yes, hi," she said.

"What's that you got there?"

"Just a duck," she said.

"Oh, well, it looks heavy. Why don't I carry it for you?"

"No, that's all right . . ."

"Please." Rick smiled his real-charmer smile. He held out his arms and Sue found herself giving up the duck.

"Taking it home?"

"Yes, for my little cousin, Carson."

"Oh, nice," Rick said and turned his real-charmer on the duck who couldn't appreciate it since its eyes were covered by the towel.

"I'd like to see the little girl's face when you give it to her," Rick said. "It's a surprise, isn't it?"

"It certainly is," Sue said. They began to walk. "You're Dinah's friend, aren't you?" She was curious about this boy of whom all the adults seemed to disapprove.

"Oh, well." Rick shrugged. "Sure," he said, "I know Dinah . . ."

"I'll be tutoring her in English."

"Yeah, great, she needs whatever help she can get, believe me."

"She mentioned that you and she were going together," Sue said.

"She did?" Rick grinned again and shook his head. "A lot of girls say that after I take 'em out a few times. I can't help that, now can I?"

"I suppose not . . ." Sue frowned.

"I guess I've been kind of playing the field . . . Looking for . . . the right kind of girl to spend most of my time with. You know?"

Sue didn't know, so she didn't answer.

"Someone," Rick continued, "I can really talk to. It's hard to find people you can really talk to."

"Quack," the duck concurred.

"You look like the kind of person people can talk to," Rick went on. "You know?"

"Me?" Sue asked.

"Yeah, I can tell. Gee, this is a big duck!"

*

"Dinah!"

"Go away, Arlette. I'm busy."

"You're not busy, Dinah, you're playing a dumb game!"

The lights and bleeps of Leon's Neon swirled around them as Dinah plunked in another quarter in the Crazy Climber game coin slot.

"Dinah, I just wanted to talk," Arlette said, leaning against the machine. "Take a break."

"Get *off*, Arlette, you're throwing the game out. Now look what you did! The pelican dropped two bombs on him and I couldn't get him out fast enough. Look out! Here comes the flower pot!"

"Dinah, stop now. Come on, let's get a Coke."

"Awwwww, look, he dropped forty stories!"

"He'll recover. I promise," Arlette sighed and took Dinah's arm.

Dinah jiggled her hand in her pocket and felt only two more quarters. "Okay," she said, "but I want to save these quarters. Will you treat me?"

"Sure," Arlette said.

They got their Cokes from a machine at the back and sat down on a bench near the office door.

Dinah popped the top of her soda can and took a hefty swig. "What'd you want to talk about?" she asked Arlette.

"Oh, nothing," Arlette shrugged. "Everything. You know. Everyone disappeared after school today. I wanted to find Claudia and maybe go shopping and then I thought about Bonnie, but she had practice—I couldn't find a soul and then I thought about you."

"Thanks a lot," Dinah grunted.

"No, I didn't mean it that way, it's just that I knew where you'd be because lately you seem to be here all the time."

"Oh, I do not."

"Yes, you do. And I just felt like talking, you know how sometimes you just feel like talking and there isn't anyone around to talk to?"

"I—"

"Sure, everybody has that feeling sometimes. And I did and there just wasn't anyone around to talk to."

"Well, I—"

"I knew you wouldn't be with Rick because I just saw him so I figured right away you'd be here, blowing your week's allowance—"

"Where?"

"Where what?"

"Where'd you see Rick, Arlette?"

"On the street. A while ago."

"He said he had to work," Dinah said.

"Well . . . maybe he was finished when I saw him with Sue."

"*What?*"

"Sue. Sue Sudley. The Stillwaters' niece, who's come to—"

"I *know* who she is. What was *Rick* doing with her?"

"He was walking. He was carrying towels and walking with her."

"Carrying towels?"

"Yeah!"

"Where were they walking?"

"I don't know," Arlette said with a wide shrug. "Toward the Stillwaters', I guess. Did you know that Mr. Coffee directed his entire English class at *me* today? I mean the en-tire class. It's my hair, don't you think? Don't you think it's terrific this way, Dinah? Mr. Coffee couldn't take his eyes off me. Oh, he's so cute! Did you see the new cheerleading outfits? I swear, the girls are going to be arrested the first time they put them on, especially Bonnie. And did you see where they sewed the megaphones? Dinah? Dinah?"

"I have to go, Arlette."

"Where?"

But Dinah had gotten up. "Do you have any money?" she asked.

"Some, why?"

"How much?"

"Five dollars, why?"

"Can I borrow it?"

"What for?"

"*Can I borrow it, Arlette?* Are you a friend or not?"

"When can you pay me back?"

"Tomorrow."

"Promise?"

"Yes, now will you just let me have it?"

Perplexed, Arlette opened her purse and dug around.

"Come *on,* Arlette," Dinah growled, and Arlette handed her a crumpled five-dollar bill.

Dinah snatched it from her hand and raced for the change girl near the Outer Space pinball machine.

"Let me have twenty quarters, Melissa," she said. The girl took the five and Dinah opened both her hands to receive the change, then struggled to stuff it all into her pockets.

"You're using my money for video games?" Arlette shrieked at Dinah, who paid no attention. Plunk! went the first quarter into Crazy Climber.

"Dinah! Dinah, listen to me, that's crazy! Why are you doing this?"

But Dinah, moving her levers, didn't hear her.

*

Paige put a bowl of steaming vegetables on the dinner table and then went again to the back door. "Carson!" she called. "Will you *please* leave that duck alone and come in and eat your supper!"

"Okay, Ma!" a faint voice called back.

"I'm sorry, Aunt Paige," Sue said. She was already seated at her place and had begun to cut Carson's pork chop for her.

"Oh, no, Sue, you were right to bring it home, poor thing. And of course, Carson was ecstatic. It's just tearing her away from it that's the hard part. And I've already told her that we've got to place an ad in the paper to try to find its owner. I'm sure she didn't listen to that part. I'll just have to reinforce that with her—"

The back door opened and Carson bounced in and leaped to her place at the table.

"Wash your hands, Carson," Nick cautioned.

"They're not dirty!"

"They're full of duck, now wash them," Paige insisted. Carson went into the downstairs bathroom and was back in four seconds.

"Let's see," Nick said and Carson held out her hands. "Honey, it doesn't do any good to just turn on the water and let your hands watch it run!"

"Oh, Daddy, hands can't *see*," Carson whined, but she washed them this time.

After the food had been dished out, Paige said, "Now remember, Carson, we did agree that we were going to

"Yeah, well, Arlette said you were here since after school."

"She gave me five and I got two from Matt—"

"—And three from me," the man in the suit said without turning around.

"Come on, Dinah," Rick said, "I'll walk you home."

"I can walk myself home," Dinah said. "You've done enough walking home for one day, haven't you?"

"Huh?"

"My sweet little tutor, Sue Sudley, you walked *her* home today, didn't you?"

Rick spread his arms and widened his eyes. "I bumped into her by accident! Outside the taproom! Honest!"

Dinah glared at him.

"It's true! I had to walk her home. The duck was heavy!"

"I heard you were carrying towels," Dinah muttered.

"The duck was *in* the towels! She couldn't have carried it that far. I took her and the duck home, watched her give the duck to her cousin and then I split! That was all!"

"Her cousin?"

"Cute little girl."

"I'll bet!"

"She's only six!"

Dinah yawned. Her arms were tired. She flexed her fingers.

"You didn't do your homework, did you?" Rick asked.

Dinah blinked.

"I didn't think so. Come on, let's get you home. But I'm dropping you off a block before. If your father sees me, I'm dead. You better tell him where you were."

"Rick?"

put an ad in the newspaper to find out just whose duck this is . . ."

"No-o-oo!" Carson wailed.

"Carson, I told you—that was the condition on which we kept it here . . ."

"I know, I know, but that was before!" Carson cried, waving her fork.

"Before what?" Paige asked.

"Before I got to know her! Before we became friends! Before she had a name!"

"What's her name?" Sue asked.

"Marcia."

"Carson, the duck probably has another name. You know, it's real owners must have given it a name . . ." Nick said.

"*I'm* her owner. And it's Marcia! Marcia, Marcia, Marcia!"

"Don't yell, Carson."

"*Please,* Ma? *Please* don't put the ad in!"

Sue reached out and touched Carson's hand. "Honey, if you love that duck so much in just one afternoon, think how its real owners must feel having lost it. You don't want them to feel so sad, never knowing what happened to their pet, do you?"

Carson pouted. "If they loved it, they wouldn't have lost it in the first place."

"Well, we don't know how it got lost," Paige said. "And we'll have to see if our ad gets answered. But we do have to place it, Carson. I'm sorry, really, but you know that's fair."

"I don't want any vegetables," Carson muttered.

"Now, then," Paige said, turning her attention to Sue. "Yes, Aunt Paige?"

"Do you have much homework tonight, Sue?"

"Not much. Why?"

"Well, I was thinking that it might be a good time for you to go over and pay a visit to Storm Ryder."

Sue took a deep breath.

"Sue, I honestly don't mean to push you, but his mother, Bunny, was over here days ago—"

"I know . . . I sent a note about the flowers . . ."

"I just thought it would be nice if you went over there and said hello. In person."

"Well, yes, except . . . I feel funny about walking in there by myself . . ."

"Why don't you go with her, Paige?" Nick suggested. "Or Carson."

"I just think it would be better if Sue went by herself. I don't want us all to barge in on Bunny and Will . . ."

"You want Sue to meet Storm. I know you," Nick said with a grin.

"Oh, please, Aunt Paige, couldn't we wait a little while?" Sue protested.

"That's her thin-lipped look," Nick said conspiratorially to Sue. "See?" He pointed. "Look how she gets."

"Don't tease me, Nick," Paige said and blushed. "Oh, Sue, won't you do this for me? And not just for me, for yourself. And Storm, too. Bunny says he just mopes around the house after school."

"But he's a boy!" Sue said.

"Yes . . ."

"Well, I feel funny, that's all. Embarrassed. I'm sure we'll meet in some natural way . . . In school, or something . . ."

"Well . . ." Paige said, "maybe I will go with you . . ."

"Oh, Aunt Paige, I'd really rather wait . . ."

"Paige, now let it be, will you?" Nick interrupted. "I've got to get back to the bar. Let Sue and Storm meet their own way, okay? They will, don't worry. Just don't push it . . ."

"All right, Nick. I'm sorry, Sue."

"I mean it, Paige, don't start in on her the moment I'm gone—"

"All *right*, Nick—"

"Bye, everybody!"

"Bye, Uncle Nick."

"Bye, Daddy."

"Bye, honey. Paige?"

"Bye, Nick . . ."

"That's better."

"And be careful of the rowdy crowd!"

*

At nine-thirty, Rick came through Leon's Neon's door. He spotted Dinah right away. She and a man in a three-piece suit playing Pac-Man were the only customers in the place. Dinah was leaning face-forward against the Crazy Climber machine.

"Dinah?" Rick said softly.

She looked up bleary-eyed.

"Your parents are going crazy, Dinah. They were worried you were running off with me or something. Your father had to work the night shift and they don't know where you are."

Dinah just looked at him.

"They called everybody—even Storm. Arlette got in touch with me. We figured you might be here."

"I'm out of money," Dinah said.

put an ad in the newspaper to find out just whose duck this is . . ."

"No-o-oo!" Carson wailed.

"Carson, I told you—that was the condition on which we kept it here . . ."

"I know, I know, but that was before!" Carson cried, waving her fork.

"Before what?" Paige asked.

"Before I got to know her! Before we became friends! Before she had a name!"

"What's her name?" Sue asked.

"Marcia."

"Carson, the duck probably has another name. You know, it's real owners must have given it a name . . ." Nick said.

"*I'm* her owner. And it's Marcia! Marcia, Marcia, Marcia!"

"Don't yell, Carson."

"*Please,* Ma? *Please* don't put the ad in!"

Sue reached out and touched Carson's hand. "Honey, if you love that duck so much in just one afternoon, think how its real owners must feel having lost it. You don't want them to feel so sad, never knowing what happened to their pet, do you?"

Carson pouted. "If they loved it, they wouldn't have lost it in the first place."

"Well, we don't know how it got lost," Paige said. "And we'll have to see if our ad gets answered. But we do have to place it, Carson. I'm sorry, really, but you know that's fair."

"I don't want any vegetables," Carson muttered.

"Now, then," Paige said, turning her attention to Sue. "Yes, Aunt Paige?"

"Do you have much homework tonight, Sue?"

"Not much. Why?"

"Well, I was thinking that it might be a good time for you to go over and pay a visit to Storm Ryder."

Sue took a deep breath.

"Sue, I honestly don't mean to push you, but his mother, Bunny, was over here days ago—"

"I know . . . I sent a note about the flowers . . ."

"I just thought it would be nice if you went over there and said hello. In person."

"Well, yes, except . . . I feel funny about walking in there by myself . . ."

"Why don't you go with her, Paige?" Nick suggested. "Or Carson."

"I just think it would be better if Sue went by herself. I don't want us all to barge in on Bunny and Will . . ."

"You want Sue to meet Storm. I know you," Nick said with a grin.

"Oh, please, Aunt Paige, couldn't we wait a little while?" Sue protested.

"That's her thin-lipped look," Nick said conspiratorially to Sue. "See?" He pointed. "Look how she gets."

"Don't tease me, Nick," Paige said and blushed. "Oh, Sue, won't you do this for me? And not just for me, for yourself. And Storm, too. Bunny says he just mopes around the house after school."

"But he's a boy!" Sue said.

"Yes . . ."

"Well, I feel funny, that's all. Embarrassed. I'm sure we'll meet in some natural way . . . In school, or something . . ."

"Well . . ." Paige said, "maybe I will go with you . . ."

"Oh, Aunt Paige, I'd really rather wait . . ."

"Paige, now let it be, will you?" Nick interrupted. "I've got to get back to the bar. Let Sue and Storm meet their own way, okay? They will, don't worry. Just don't push it . . ."

"All right, Nick. I'm sorry, Sue."

"I mean it, Paige, don't start in on her the moment I'm gone—"

"All *right,* Nick—"

"Bye, everybody!"

"Bye, Uncle Nick."

"Bye, Daddy."

"Bye, honey. Paige?"

"Bye, Nick . . ."

"That's better."

"And be careful of the rowdy crowd!"

*

At nine-thirty, Rick came through Leon's Neon's door. He spotted Dinah right away. She and a man in a three-piece suit playing Pac-Man were the only customers in the place. Dinah was leaning face-forward against the Crazy Climber machine.

"Dinah?" Rick said softly.

She looked up bleary-eyed.

"Your parents are going crazy, Dinah. They were worried you were running off with me or something. Your father had to work the night shift and they don't know where you are."

Dinah just looked at him.

"They called everybody—even Storm. Arlette got in touch with me. We figured you might be here."

"I'm out of money," Dinah said.

"Yeah, well, Arlette said you were here since after school."

"She gave me five and I got two from Matt—"

"—And three from me," the man in the suit said without turning around.

"Come on, Dinah," Rick said, "I'll walk you home."

"I can walk myself home," Dinah said. "You've done enough walking home for one day, haven't you?"

"Huh?"

"My sweet little tutor, Sue Sudley, you walked *her* home today, didn't you?"

Rick spread his arms and widened his eyes. "I bumped into her by accident! Outside the taproom! Honest!"

Dinah glared at him.

"It's true! I had to walk her home. The duck was heavy!"

"I heard you were carrying towels," Dinah muttered.

"The duck was *in* the towels! She couldn't have carried it that far. I took her and the duck home, watched her give the duck to her cousin and then I split! That was all!"

"Her cousin?"

"Cute little girl."

"I'll bet!"

"She's only six!"

Dinah yawned. Her arms were tired. She flexed her fingers.

"You didn't do your homework, did you?" Rick asked.

Dinah blinked.

"I didn't think so. Come on, let's get you home. But I'm dropping you off a block before. If your father sees me, I'm dead. You better tell him where you were."

"Rick?"

"What?"

"Did she really have a duck too heavy for her to carry?"

"Yeah, she really did."

Dinah sighed. "Okay, honey. I'll go home now."

— ✳ —

The last Friday
in September . . .

Lost in thought, Sue walked through the Palatine High halls clutching her books to her chest and looking straight ahead. She didn't hear her name being called until Mr. Coffee was almost on top of her.

"Sue, didn't you hear me calling you?" he asked, taking her shoulders in his hands. "Are you all right?"

"Yes," Sue said and smiled. "I'm all right, Mr. Coffee, I was just thinking about Dinah. She hasn't come to the last tutoring sessions I set up with her. I was there and I waited and waited, but she never came."

"Mmmmm . . ."

"I'm worried about her. I tried to catch her between classes to talk to her about it, but she seems to disappear as soon as I get near her."

"Well." Mr. Coffee took his hands from Sue's shoulders. "I think I'd better have a talk with her. I'm afraid she's going to flunk if she doesn't get down to work fast."

"That's what *I* was afraid of," Sue said.

"How many sessions have you had with her?" Mr. Coffee asked.

"Well, I've set up six," Sue answered.

"And how many has she attended?"

"One."

"I see . . ."

"I really don't know what to do. Somehow, I feel responsible."

"You're not responsible, my dear," Mr. Coffee said. "Don't you even think that. You've done everything you can. I'll talk to Dinah now. My, that is a lovely sweater . . ."

"Thank you."

"And the skirt's pretty, too."

"Thank you."

"The boots go nicely with it."

"Thank you."

"And by the way, there's a meeting of the newspaper staff this afternoon, Sue . . ."

"Thank you. I mean, yes, all right, I'll be there . . ."

"Oh, good. Two-twenty, Room 201. See you then."

*

"Hi, Sue!"

"Oh, hi, Arlette . . ."

"I guess your being here means you're joining the newspaper staff now, right?"

Sue smiled. "Yes, I guess so."

"That's terrific, I mean it, just terrific. I love the newspaper, it's so much fun and you get to meet so many people. Mr. Coffee's a wonderful advisor, you know, he's not heavyhanded or anything, he lets us put in practically everything we want. Did you see how he kept looking at my new hairdo? Oh, look, here comes Matt. Hi, Matt! You remember Matt Argus, Sue, didn't I introduce you to him at Leon's Neon? He does sports mostly. There's Bonnie, I have to go say hello to Bonnie, see you in a minute, Sue . . ."

Sue shook her head dizzily as Arlette trailed off after

Bonnie. Absently she picked up a copy of *The Palatine Prattler* lying in a pile on one of the desks. It had been the first issue of the year and was only two pages. She was reading a poem written by one of the students called "Summer Dies," when she felt someone standing behind her and she looked up quickly.

"Awful isn't it," a tall boy said with a smile.

"The poem?"

"Yeah. 'Summer Dies.' Phew! But nobody else contributed any poems. Coffee always likes us to include at least one poem. You're new, aren't you?"

"Yes," Sue replied. "I'm Sue Sudley."

"Oh, right!" the boy said. "Someone told me about you. You're living with your aunt, right? Sorry about what happened to your parents."

"Thank you," Sue said softly. "I guess word gets around fast in Palatine, doesn't it?"

"Fast? It streaks. No secrets in a town like this. My name is Roger Gurney. I'm the editor."

"Oh! The editor!"

"Impressive, isn't it? Not really, but my father is Roger Gurney Sr. He's the editor of the town paper, the *Palatine P.M.-Daily* and so everybody expects me to follow in his footsteps."

"Oh, but that's not right," Sue said. "You shouldn't have to do anything just because your father does it."

Roger Gurney smiled. "I know. That's my little cop-out. Actually, I want to be a journalist. Better than my father!"

"Is he very good?"

"No."

"Okay, people, we're all here, let's begin . . . Roger?" Mr. Coffee stepped away from the desk at the front of the room and Roger Gurney, carrying a sheaf of papers, took his place. He smiled briefly at Sue before he spoke.

"I have some of the stories you've submitted for the next issue, and by the way I hope you know the deadline is two weeks from today. That soccer story is good, Matt, but I'd like you to rewrite it a little more positively."

"But we lost our first five games!" Matt said.

"I know, but I don't think it'll help morale to point out that—well, let me quote here—" He dug through the papers and found the one he wanted—"to point out that 'with this crummy team I predict we'll lose the next thirteen, too!' "

"Oh," Matt said. "Well . . . I guess I see what you mean."

"Good."

"It's true, though."

"Never mind, Matt. And Arlette, your gossip column is fine, but leave out the teachers."

"But, Roger—"

"No teachers."

"But—"

"And it's all good fun to write about 'who was seen with who,' but you don't have to go into detail about what they were seen *doing*."

"But Rog—"

"No details, Arlette. And I was thinking that perhaps instead of gossip next issue, you might enjoy doing a story about new arrivals at our school."

"You mean—"

"I mean new faculty members or maybe . . . new students. Introduce them to everyone. In the newspaper. What do you think, Arlette?"

"Well, I—"

"Good. Kevin, that was a nice drawing of Diane Keaton you did to accompany your movie review."

"Thanks, Rog."

"—Except Diane Keaton wasn't in the movie."

"She wasn't?"

"No. Didn't you see it?"

"Well, actually . . . I was sick the night I was supposed to go. Jane Lowenstein told me about it."

"Jane Lowenstein was putting you on, Kevin. I'm appalled that you really didn't see the movie you reviewed, but equally appalled that it's a pretty interesting review. Can you do a drawing of Meryl Streep?"

"Was she in the movie?"

"Yes, she was."

"Oh. Well, Diane Keaton is the only movie star I can draw. Wait, I can do a pretty good Barbra Streisand . . ."

"Forget it. We'll run something else. Now, about the editorial . . ." Roger paused and studied the faces of his staff. He took a deep breath. "I know this will probably be an unpopular idea," he began, "but I think editorials are meant to stir up some controversy, get people talking, that kind of thing . . ." He looked over at Mr. Coffee, but the teacher showed no reaction.

"I agree, Roger," Bonnie Finster said eagerly, wiggling in her seat, "and I have a terrific idea for—"

"Bonnie, I'm sorry, you're out of order," Roger interrupted. "Let me finish and then you can present your idea, okay?"

"Oh. Sure." Bonnie twitched her shoulders and smiled prettily at Roger.

"As I was saying," Roger continued, "I know this

might be unpopular, but it's important. It's about the video games center in town—Leon's Neon." There was a scattering of applause around the room. "That's just the kind of thing I mean," Roger said, frowning. "These video games aren't just a pasttime anymore. For some kids, they're a way of life!" There was more applause. "Now cut that out!" Roger said. "Don't you see? They're insidious in their own way. Not only because of all the money the kids spend—*waste*—on them, all those quarters down the slot—but because they're so time-and-mind wasting as well!" The room became silent. "Nobody's reading books or working or studying or anything anymore. Everybody in Palatine is at Leon's Neon!"

"Well, gee, Roger, are you saying we're supposed to spend all our time reading or studying or something?" Arlette pouted. "I mean, what about fun, Roger?"

"Yeah, now look, Rog," Matt Argus said, "we all know you're a big brain and going to take over *The New York Times* someday and all that, but some of us are just plain kids, you know?"

Roger sighed. "All I mean," he said, "is that there should be moderation. There's nothing wrong with video games, really, except when they take over completely. And that's what I think has happened since Leon's Neon opened. I know some games are good for coordination and that there are other good things about them, too, besides being fun. But just think about it: during lunch, after school—*where is everybody?*" He paused and looked at the staffers. None was looking back at him. They were all staring at their desks or at the floor.

"Ah, well, that certainly does seem to be a controversial subject, Roger—" Mr. Coffee said hesitantly.

"We could back it with a story," Roger went on. "One of us could spend some time down there and write what he observes. You know, pick kids at random and watch them: how much time and money they spend—"

Silence.

"Can I say my idea now, Roger?" Bonnie asked brightly.

Roger sighed. "Sure," he said.

Bonnie stood up and smoothed her sweater. *"Well,"* she began, "you all know that we're putting together our winter Olympics program now, right?" There was some applause for the winter Olympics program, especially from Matt. "Yeah, it's going to be just great. My squad is ready to cheer its little heart out! But what I think we should let everyone know about—and this *is* controversial, too, Roger—" she said, putting on her serious look, "is the decision the office made about the Brazilian flag."

"What Brazilian flag?" someone asked.

"See?" Bonnie said, spreading her arms. "No one knows about it. That's why it should be in the paper. You know Rosaria Anduvar?"

"The exchange student from Brazil?"

"That's the one. Well, she's competing this year and she's just terrific, I mean terrific! And when we have the Olympics, some of us decided that it would just be so democratic and all to wave a Brazilian flag *in addition* to the Palatine High flag and the American flag!" Bonnie finished, clasped her hands together and beamed at her little audience.

Sue, who had been silent throughout the meeting, blinked her eyes. She had been waiting for Bonnie's point and was surprised because Bonnie seemed to have made it. But as she looked at Roger and Mr. Coffee and the others, they seemed to be waiting, too.

Finally, Matt expressed what the others were thinking. He turned to Bonnie, opened his palms and bellowed, "SO?"

"Well, don't you see?" Bonnie asked, bewildered. "The office said *no!* No! We couldn't spend twelve dollars to buy the Brazilian flag! Now isn't that just terrible? Shouldn't the students have a voice in that? I mean, maybe everyone would want to chip in, or we could have a raffle, or—"

"Bonnie," Roger interrupted. "You mean you want to have an editorial on the school buying a flag for the Olympics? Is that what you're saying?"

"Well, yes, Roger. I mean, I really believe that the school paper should deal with school stuff, not this heavy kind of stuff you want, telling the kids that the way they spend their leisure time is silly. I mean, that's none of your business, Roger, really!"

Roger looked at Sue who returned a sympathetic smile.

"Bonnie's right, Roger," Arlette said. "I think your idea's a turnoff. Maybe there are some kids who do spend too much time down at Leon's, but not all of them—"

"Too many, Arlette," Roger said. "And not just here, either, it's all over. And what do they do when they go home? They play the games on their TVs. It's like designer jeans, Arlette. There's just too much emphasis on stuff like that. And that's where everybody's money goes, don't you see?"

Arlette automatically slapped a hand over the label on the back of her jeans.

Mr. Coffee turned in his seat. "Sue," he said, "you

haven't said a word during this meeting. You're part of our staff now. Let's hear what you think."

Sue opened her mouth but closed it again as Arlette beamed an encouraging "Yeah!"

"Don't be influenced, Sue," Roger said. "What *do* you think?"

Sue pursed her lips and then spoke tentatively. "I—I think—" she began.

"It's okay, Sue," Mr. Coffee said with a nod. "Be honest. Speak your mind."

"Uh, well, I don't want to make anyone angry," she said, "but I do think that as far as the flag is concerned, those who are interested in waving one could chip in on their own or someone could even sew one!"

Everyone was staring at her now and she moved her fingers nervously.

"Well . . . Betsy Ross did it . . ." she said lamely.

"What are you saying, Sue?" Roger said.

"Only that I think that Roger's idea could start everyone talking. As he said. And that's good, even though there might be some real arguments about it. Arguments make people think, after all . . . And isn't that what a good newspaper should do?"

Arlette made a face. "I think a school newspaper should just be fun," she mumbled.

"It could be a combination, Arlette," Sue said.

"Good for you, Sue," Roger whispered with a smile. He didn't know if she heard him.

Mr. Coffee turned to Arlette. "Don't you agree," he said, "that making people think and talk is the only way to make things happen?"

Arlette basked in the sudden attention from the teacher.

"Yes," she said breathily.

"I think so, too. Roger, you write the editorial and to whom would you assign the story?" Out of the corner of his eye, Mr. Coffee glanced at Sue.

"Well, how about Sue?" Roger said.

"Me? Oh, not me, someone who's been on the staff a while should—"

"No, I think you should do it, Sue. After all, you were the only one who agreed with the idea . . . I'm giving you the assignment. You'll have to spend some time down there and really see what's going on."

Matt turned around in his seat to face Sue. "Listen, Sue, while you're down there, why don't you make a list of the high-scorers for the sports page?" he said, but Roger glared at him.

*

Sue's mind was full of the newspaper meeting when she arrived home, but the loud quacking she heard pulled her out of her reverie. Clutching her books, she raced for the back yard, where she found Carson with one hand around the duck's neck and the other force-feeding a brown mush into the duck's beak with a plastic spoon. Tears were streaming down Carson's tiny face and Sue noticed the duck wasn't amused either.

"Carson!" she cried, hurrying over and kneeling down next to the little girl. "Carson, stop! Stop, honey—" She took the hand that was squeezing the duck's neck. "Carson, that's not the way to feed her, honey—"

"But she won't eat, Cousin Sue," Carson sobbed. "She hasn't eaten all day! I just wanted to make her eat or she'll die . . ." She broke into fresh sobs.

"Oh, Carson, come on now, she'll be all right . . ."

Sue picked up the doll's bowl that Carson had filled with the brown mush.

"Carson, what is this?" she asked, sniffing it.

"Friskies Buffet." Carson snuffled and wiped her face with the back of her hand.

"Cat food?"

"Well, that's what she's been eating since we got her . . . We had lots of cans left over from when we had a cat. Before you came. He got run over."

"Aw, I'm sorry . . ."

"So I've been feeding her the cans and she seemed to like it up till today . . . I don't want her to die, Cousin Sue . . ."

"She won't die, honey, she won't die. Tell you what: Why don't I take her to the vet? I'll bet that there's some special food ducks are supposed to eat and we'll find out what it is, okay? Is Mom in the house?"

Carson shook her head. "No, she's been out all day. Mrs. Ryder's supposed to be taking care of me till you got home, but she can see me from her kitchen window."

"Do you know where the vet's office is?" Sue asked. "Can I walk there from here?"

"Oh, sure, it's before you get to all the stores. It's on Appleby, two blocks over that way and one block over that way. I know exactly where it is because I used to go over there all the time while our cat was getting better from being run over."

"Oh, your cat got better?"

"Yeah, he got better from being run over but after that he ran away. Why don't I go with you and show you because you might get lost if I just tell you."

"All right. I'll get a leash for the duck and you tell Mrs. Ryder I'll watch you now."

*

The receptionist frowned when she peered over her desk and saw that the animal on the end of the leash wasn't a dog.

"Is it housebroken?" she sniffed.

"No," Carson said, "but its doodoo is small."

"Dr. Krass will see you very shortly," the receptionist said. "I'll get him!"

She hurried through a door to the examining room.

"Where's your mom today, Carson?" Sue asked, bending down to stroke Marcia.

"I don't know." Carson shrugged. "She said she had a lot to do."

"I left a note on the kitchen table telling her where we were. Did she say when she'd be—"

Sue was interrupted by a stocky, bearded man in a white coat.

"Yes, you have a duck," he said, nodding so deeply toward Sue and Carson he seemed to be bowing.

"Quack," the duck confirmed and snapped at the doctor's coat.

"Ducks are terrible pets. They're rude, noisy, unbelievably messy, and they're totally unresponsive to affection."

"So are you!" Carson declared and stuck out her tongue.

Dr. Krass ignored her. "I'm just trying to tell you what you're letting yourself in for. What seems to be wrong with it?"

"It doesn't want to eat," Sue said.

"Ah, well." The vet turned to his receptionist. "Emily, why don't you get a plastic sheet over here until I'm ready . . ." As the woman went into the back rooms again, Dr. Krass turned to Sue. "I'll take you as soon as I can, but I've got a rhesus monkey back there with a swollen jaw. And he had an appointment."

"Oh, I'm sorry about the monkey—" Sue said.

"Monkeys are rude. The rudest, next to ducks," the doctor growled and went into the back, just as the receptionist came out with a large sheet of plastic which she spread over half the waiting room floor.

Sue herded Marcia over to the sheet and was just about to sit down when there was a tapping at the outside door. The receptionist called "It's open!" and went back to her filing. At the sound of more tapping, Sue opened the door herself. Facing her was a boy about her own age in an orange wheelchair, holding a large nondescript dog on a leash.

"Hi," the boy said to Sue and smiled shyly. "I couldn't quite manage the door and the dog, too . . ."

The dog leaped up against Sue and wrapped his front paws around her waist.

"Knuckles!" the boy said sharply and yanked on the leash. The dog calmed down.

"That's why I've brought him here," the boy explained, wheeling in. "He's getting impossible. Uncontrollable. Thanks for holding the door."

"You're welcome," Sue said and quickly bent to untangle the leash from the wheel of the chair.

"Quack!" Marcia screamed when she saw the dog, and flew two feet into the air.

"ARRRRGH!" Knuckles answered, diving for Marcia. The boy tugged sharply at the leash, forcing the wheelchair back. Sue grabbed for it as it was about to tip and Carson scooped up the duck on the other side of the room. Emily, the receptionist continued to file.

"It's all right, I've got you," Sue said, righting the wheelchair.

"Thanks—Sit, Knuckles, *sit!*" the boy cried. The dog reluctantly sat, panting and grunting. Carson sat, too, with the big duck in her lap. Sue straightened her skirt and walked around the wheelchair to face the boy.

"Hi, I'm Irwin Ryder," he offered and held out his hand.

Sue took it. "Storm?" she asked hesitantly.

"Oh. Yeah," he grinned. "Storm. They started calling me that when I—when I—"

"Well, it's a change from Irwin," Sue said quickly.

"Big change, yeah," he said, still grinning. "My mother brought me over here . . . She wanted to come in with me, but I wanted to handle this on my own because Knuckles is my dog. Guess I should have let her . . ."

"Oh, no," Sue said. "It was only that you didn't know there'd be a duck in here. You can handle your dog. And I'm Sue Sudley, your next door neighbor."

Storm's jaw dropped. "Really? Wow, what a way to meet. Guess I should have come over or something, but—"

"It's perfectly all right. I should have come over to see you, too, but I've been—well, kind of recovering from—"

"Me, too. Recovering," Storm said.

"I'm so glad we met after all," Sue said.

"Oh, me too, me too!" They both smiled at each other.

"Well . . ." Sue said.

"Well . . ." Storm said.

"Guess I'll sit down," Sue said.

"Me, too," Storm said and laughed. "Well . . . recovering sure isn't easy, is it?"

"No, it isn't," Sue replied as the office door opened.

Marcia quacked ominously and Knuckles growled as Dr. Krass came out.

"Hello, there, Storm. What's wrong with Knuckles?" he asked.

"We think he's a manic-depressive, Dr. Krass," Storm explained. "He behaves wildly with everybody but the family, and when he's at home he just lies with his nose in his paws."

"Mmmmm," the vet mused. "Well, I'll get rid of the duck first and then we'll have a look at him."

Carson stuck her tongue out at the vet again as Sue lifted Marcia from the little girl's lap and they followed Dr. Krass into the examining room.

When they emerged, a woman was sitting on the couch next to Storm's chair.

"Oh, Sue, this is my mother," Storm said. "Mom, this is Sue Sudley, Mrs. Stillwater's niece."

Bunny Ryder stood up and held out her hand, but Sue's arms were full of Marcia.

"It's nice to meet you, Mrs. Ryder," Sue said.

"It's lovely to meet *you* at last, Sue. I didn't know you and Carson were coming here, too. I could have driven you when Carson told me—"

"We managed all right—" Sue said, but Mrs. Ryder went on.

"If you don't mind waiting until Dr. Krass sees Knuckles, I'll be glad to take you home. I have the wagon and it won't be any trouble at all."

"Thank you," Sue said. "That would be nice."

"What'd he say about the duck?" Storm asked after the vet had gone back with Knuckles and Mrs. Ryder.

"Just that we've probably been feeding her wrong. There are duck pellets we can buy or—" Sue took a piece of paper out of her pocket and glanced at it—"get her a mixture of corn meal, bran and rolled oats."

"And dry milk and salt and cod liver oil and table scraps," Carson piped.

"Boy," Storm said, shaking his head. "Ducks are harder than dogs."

"And you can't paper train them," Sue added. "I guess my aunt and uncle will probably want to find it a home."

"Sure. It's going to need water . . . a lake or something . . . and there's nothing too close to our houses like that."

"Mmmm," Sue agreed.

"We're keeping the duck," Carson said firmly.

*

The offices of the *Palatine P.M.-Daily* consisted of two small storefront rooms plus the presses in the back. Roger Gurney Sr. occupied most of the editorial office, standing six-three, weighing about two hundred and fifty pounds, and cramming all this behind a desk that was once the front door of the high school gymnasium. He enjoyed wearing a green eyeshade like the ones the editors wore in the comics he'd read as a child, and now he peered up through it to find his son, Roger Jr., standing at the front of his desk.

"Rog!" he said heartily. "What a nice surprise! Have a seat!"

"Where?"

"Oh . . . well . . ."

"It's okay, Dad, I don't need to sit. I just wanted to tell you that we're going to go ahead with that piece on the video games. The one I told you about, remember?"

"Sure, I remember. I didn't think they'd go along with you, though."

"Well, they nearly didn't. But now, not only are we doing the editorial, I've got someone backing it up with a story, too!"

Roger Sr. leaned back in his chair and the wood floor groaned.

"Now who'd you get to write a story like that? Your whining sports editor or that dippy gossip girl?"

"Come on, Dad, it's not professional to knock a rival paper to its face. No, not anyone you know. She's— She's new in town. And she's just terrific, Dad, I mean really . . . really terrific! She's the one who backed me on the idea. And she's going down to Leon's Neon to do the research for the follow-up piece."

"New in town, eh? Who is she?"

"Her name's Sue Sudley."

"*Who?*"

"Sue Sudley. You know the Stillwaters? Dad?"

Roger Gurney Sr. pulled out a large blue handkerchief and mopped his forehead. "I know the Stillwaters," he said.

"She's their niece. She lost her parents recently. She's living with them."

"I wrote the obit about her parents," Roger's father said softly. "I caught the story on the telex . . . Midair collision . . . She came from here . . ."

"Who, Sue?"

"Her mother."

Roger Jr. looked at his father whose eyes were tightly closed now. "Dad?" he said.

"Freshman prom queen. Pretty thing. Pretty . . ."

"Dad?"

"Had this blue dress. Like gauze. Periwinkle blue . . ."

"Dad?"

Roger Sr. opened his eyes. "The daughter, you said? Living with Paige Stillwater?"

The boy nodded.

"Can she write?"

"I'm betting on it."

Roger Sr. stood up, towering over his son. "Tell you what, Rog," he said, "you do a good story and maybe I'll run it in the *Daily*."

"Yeah?"

"The big time, kid."

"My piece and Sue's, too? Both of them?"

"Why not?"

Roger Jr. wagged his head. "This is some girl, Dad. I knew it right off!"

*

As Sue and Carson and Marcia got out of the Ryders' station wagon, Mrs. Ryder touched Sue's arm.

"Are you busy this evening, Sue, dear?" she asked.

"I have some homework, but not more than an hour of it. Why?"

Mrs. Ryder glanced at Storm, then turned back to Sue.

"I was wondering if you'd like to come over. When you're finished. Maybe you and Storm could play . . .

Scrabble. Or something. Get to know your neighbor, as they say . . ."

"Yeah, Sue, could you?" Storm asked softly. "I'd like that."

"Of course. I'd love to," Sue answered, thinking Aunt Paige would be so pleased. And it did happen naturally, just as she'd preferred. "Thank you," she said, "for the invitation and the lift."

"Quack," Marcia said, and Carson added, "Quack!"

*

"*Xyloid!*" Sue cried. "That's terrific, Storm! And on a triple word score, too! I'll never catch up now."

Storm waved his hand at her. "Don't complain to me. Not after you went out in the last game with *zoology!* That was mind-blowing."

Sue laughed. "This was fun, Storm. I'm glad I came over."

"Yeah, I'm glad, too."

"That's some sharp chair you've got."

"The kids bought it for me. They all chipped in, the team, the cheerleaders, friends . . . See the alligator on the backrest?"

"They must like you an awful lot."

"Yeah, well, that was when I was carrying the ball for good old Palatine Junior High. I'm not much use now . . ."

Sue frowned at him. "Don't try to tell me that everyone only liked you for your football playing, Storm. Anybody who knows the word 'xyloid' is smarter than to think something like that."

Storm tried to smile. "I really feel disoriented, Sue.

Sometimes I don't know where I am or what I'm even doing here. Nothing's the same as it was."

Sue nodded. "I know just what you mean. Lots of times I feel the same way."

"I look at my friends differently. I keep wondering what they're thinking."

"Are they feeling sorry for me? Are they just being nice out of pity?" Sue added.

"Exactly!" Storm leaned forward in his chair. "I'm never really sure. And besides that, I feel changed inside as well as out."

"I know. My outside life is different now but so is my inside life," Sue said.

"Yeah," Storm whispered.

They looked at each other.

— ✳ —

After school,
three days later . . .

Rick blew in her left ear and Bonnie squealed shrilly.

"Sh!" he said, looking around. "Keep it down, Bonnie, I don't want anyone seeing us . . ." They were crouched under the bleachers of the football field.

"No one's around at all, Rick," Bonnie said. "No one's even jogging. Relax!"

"Hey, that's *my* line, baby," Rick said, trying for her right ear this time. Suddenly Bonnie pulled away sharply and Rick banged his nose on a post.

"Hey-y!" he whined, cupping his hand over his nose.

"Someone *was* here," Bonnie said, peering under the benches.

"Did you see them?"

"No. I could just feel it, that's all," she told him. "I feel these things, Rick, I'm very sensitive."

"I know, baby," Rick said, grabbing for her again, but she pushed her hand against his chest.

"No, Rick, I'm not kidding. Somebody was here." She began to nibble a long red fingernail. "Do you know what Dinah did to me the last time she heard we were together?"

"What?"

"She put talcum powder inside my blowdryer, and when I took it out of my gym locker—"

"I remember that," Rick interrupted. "I saw you. Your whole head was white."

"You bet it was. I wanted to do something really nasty back, except Arlette made me swear not to, since she was the one who told me it was Dinah."

"Dinah gets a little crazy where I'm concerned," Rick said.

"Yeah, but I'm the one who pays for it," Bonnie pouted.

"Naw, you're not the only one," Rick said. "Lisa Caplow got her hair pulled, Elizabeth Rainey had her bra stolen, Candy Seidle got her homework glued together, Mary Jo Birch had her shoelaces—"

"Thanks, Rick, thanks a lot," Bonnie said and rolled her eyes.

*

Dinah leaned against the Crazy Climber machine and scanned the room. A little boy reached for the machine's slot, his outstretched hand clutching a quarter and Dinah moved quickly, stepping in to block him.

"Machine's taken, sonny," she said.

"You're not playing it," the boy said.

"I'm taking a break. Go play something else."

"You can't do that," the boy whined.

"Yes I can. I own this machine," Dinah announced.

"Really?"

"Really. But we have no room for it at home, so I board it here."

The boy made a face, shrugged and walked away.

Dinah looked around again for someone who'd lend her a quarter and spotted Arlette heading for her. She tried to hide but it was too late. Arlette came gushing up.

"Still playing, Dinah? I think Roger was talking about you at the last *Prattler* meeting we had."

"Talking about me?"

"Yes. About the kids who never study and spend all their time and money on video games. Like an addiction, or something . . ."

"Don't be silly," Dinah sniffed. "I can stop any time I want to."

"Mmmm."

"Lend me a quarter, Arlette?"

"Okay . . ." She tossed one and Dinah grabbed for it hungrily.

"Where's Rick lately?" Arlette asked, as Dinah, her pupils dilating, began to play the game.

"I'm sure you know," Dinah said without looking up.

"I do. Behind the bleachers, breathing on Bonnie."

"Ooooooooh!" Dinah screeched, and tilted the machine.

"Well, we're friends, I thought you'd want to know," Arlette said. "I'm a believer in honesty, even if other people aren't. Oh, there's Sue. Gee, this is the first time I've seen her here since I brought her in the first week of school . . ." Arlette drifted away from Dinah who was still shaking the Crazy Climber, and moved over to Sue.

"Hi, Sue!" Arlette bubbled.

"Oh, hi, Arlette . . ."

"You look a little dazed. Deciding what to play first? Or are you looking for someone? I can tell you where everyone is . . ."

"No . . . thanks, Arlette . . . I'm here for my story. You know, the one Roger assigned me?"

Arlette snapped her fingers. "Of course! I forgot you were the one for a minute. Well, I've got your story for you."

"You do?"

"I sure do." Sue followed Arlette's eyes and spotted Dinah slumped against the Crazy Climber machine, banging her head.

"It's Dinah!" Sue said.

"It's Dinah," Arlette concurred.

"What's wrong with her?"

"Everything. She's a real mess."

"I guess I'll go talk to her," Sue said. "She hasn't kept any appointments for tutoring since the first one."

"Do you have any quarters?" Arlette asked.

"Quarters? Why?"

"Because she'll only talk to you if you keep feeding her quarters. Kind of like the seals at the zoo."

"See you later, Arlette," Sue said and went over to Dinah, who was rubbing her head.

"Hi, Dinah . . ." she began.

"Lend me a quarter, Sue?" Dinah pleaded.

"Okay . . . But can I ask you something first?"

"No. First the quarter."

Sue sighed and handed her one.

"Dinah, how come you haven't let me help you in English? We made so many appointments . . . Why didn't you show up?"

"I thought I'd give you time to be with Rick," Dinah said. The machine's music beeped the theme from *The Pink Panther*.

"Rick? *Me?*" Sue asked.

"I heard about your little walk," Dinah said, trying body English on the machine. "You. And Rick. And the towels."

"Towels?" She frowned. "Oh! The time he took my duck home!"

Dinah looked up for the first time and her eyes were softer.

"Then that was really true? About the duck?"

Sue looked blank. "True that Rick carried my duck home for me? Yes . . ."

Dinah squealed. "Seventy-six thousand points! My best game!" She caressed the side of the machine. "I wanted to believe him, but it was kind of hard. He tells me one thing and then I hear something completely different. Can I have another quarter, Sue?"

Sue took a quarter out of her purse. Dinah lunged for it but Sue pulled her hand away.

"Dinah, you can have it, but you have to promise you'll keep an appointment with me. For tutoring."

Again, Dinah reached for the coin, but Sue stepped back further.

"Promise," Sue said firmly.

Dinah wailed, "For only *one* quarter?"

"Dinah, you need the help or you'll flunk!" Sue cried.

"What do *you* care," Dinah muttered. "You don't even know me."

"You don't have to know someone well to want to help," Sue said.

"A dollar," Dinah said. "Four quarters."

"One."

"Two? Two quarters?"

"One."

"O-*kay.*"

Sue watched Dinah play her game. Dinah's eyes were small slits. Her mouth hung open and she kept running her tongue back and forth against her upper lip.

"Dinah?" Sue said.

"Sh!"

"Dinah, how about tomorrow afternoon?"

"Sh!"

"Dinah, you promised!"

"Sh!"

"Dinah, stop it!"

Dinah stopped because the game was over and she lost.

"One more quarter and I'll go to two sessions!" she said to Sue.

"Dinah," Sue said, "you're hooked on video games."

"I'm not. I'm not really. I don't have to do this. It's just a social thing. You know . . . a social thing? I'm not hooked. I'm not."

"Okay, then," Sue said, and she took out her notebook and a pencil.

"What's that?" Dinah asked suspiciously.

"Don't worry, I'm just making some notes. I promise not to use your name, but I'm doing a story for *The Prattler* on kids who spend all their time and money here at Leon's." She saw Dinah frown. "I'm telling you because I don't want you to think I'm doing anything behind your back. Honest, Dinah, I won't mention your name. Now tell me something: Do you only play the games after school? Or do you need to play one in the morning, too?"

"Well . . . sometimes. Sometimes in the morning I need to play before I get to school . . ."

"Do you ever cut school to play?"

"No!"

"Dinah?"

"Sometimes."

Poor Dinah, Sue thought, as she made her notes. She's so young to be hooked this way. If I do my story on her, maybe I'll be able to learn a way to help her at the same time . . .

*

Sue heard the scream from inside the house as she was coming up the walk, her head still full of Dinah, electric lights, bleeps, bongs, buzzes and the theme from *The Pink Panther*. But all of that was forgotten at the sound of that horrible cry and she raced for the front door.

"*WWWAAAAAAAHHHHH!*" came the second scream and this time it was followed by harsh, choked sobs. It was coming from upstairs.

Sue flung her jacket and books on the couch and was headed for the stairs when Paige wandered into the living room from the kitchen.

"*WAAAHHHH!*"

"Aunt Paige," Sue said breathlessly, "what are you doing down here? What's going on up there, what's—"

"Oh," Paige said casually, "that's just Carson."

"*WAAAAAAHHHHHHHHHHHH!*"

"But—but Aunt Paige, she—"

"She's having a tantrum because we got a call this afternoon about the duck. I've talked to her, but I had to send her to her room when she started screaming. Four, three, two—"

"*WAAAAAHHHHH!*"

"It's about a count of fourteen before she builds up to another one," Paige said.

"Oh!" Sue put her palm to her chest and relaxed. "It sounded like she was being murdered!"

"I know. She'll be all right in about another seven minutes. Let's go into the kitchen, where it won't be so disturbing. Oh, I nearly forgot to tell you. Storm called while you were out. He'll call back. Where were you?"

"I went down to Leon's Neon. I'm doing a story for the school paper about the kids who hang out there," Sue explained. "There's one girl in particular who's really in trouble. Dinah Deener."

"Oh, yes. It's that Rick. Benita says her grades have gone down badly."

"It's worse than that. She's addicted to those games. She's a Crazy Climber junkie. Did Storm say what he wanted?"

"No," Paige said with a small smile. "But I think he's very fond of you."

"I like him, too. I can see why he's so popular. By the way, who called about the duck?"

"Oh, it's a family from town, but no one we know. Mr. and Mrs. Hegelmeyer. They have a little boy who's been heartbroken since the duck got away. It seems he always tried to sneak the duck into the house while his parents weren't looking, and this time he was nearly caught, so he left the duck at the side of the house with a big bowl of food, thinking it would stay there while he distracted his mother."

"And that's when the duck wandered off?"

"Yes, by the time the boy got back the duck was gone. They were thrilled to see the ad."

"Are you sure it's the same duck?"

"They seemed pretty sure. They're coming by tonight, some time after dinner."

"Poor Carson . . ."

"Carson will have to bear up," Paige said. "Maybe we'll get her a hamster . . ."

The phone rang and Paige answered it.

"For you," she said, holding out the receiver to Sue. "It's a boy. I think it's Storm."

"Oh, good," Sue said. "Hello?"

"Sue? Hi, this is Roger."

"Roger?"

"Roger Gurney. From the paper? Roger Gurney Jr.?"

"Of course. I'm sorry, Roger, I thought at first you were—"

"Who?"

"Someone else. I'm glad you called though, because I wanted to tell you you were right about those games. I went to Leon's Neon this afternoon, and while not all kids are that bad, there's one who's really hooked on them. Her schoolwork's gone down the tubes, she owes a fortune in quarters and you should see her eyes!"

"Wow, that sounds like a good story, Sue."

"Well, yes, but it's more than that. This girl's in trouble!"

"Listen, Sue, I had an idea. Why don't we get together tonight and work on it. The story, I mean. Suppose I pick you up at about seven-thirty and we'll go downtown, maybe drop in at Leon's to see what's happening and then get a bite to eat and talk about it. Decide what your lead should be."

"Uh—"

"Okay?"

"Just a minute . . ." Sue put her hand over the

mouthpiece. "Aunt Paige? Is it all right if I go out with Roger tonight to work on my story for the paper?"

"Roger *Gurney?*"

"Uh huh."

"He's taking you out to work on a story?"

"Yes. Is it all right?"

"He operates just like his father," Paige mumbled.

"What?"

"Nothing. Certainly you can go if you like, dear, but be home by ten."

"I will. Yes, Roger," she said. "Seven-thirty will be fine!" She hung up and turned to Paige. "Aunt Paige, I'm going to go up and talk to Carson, okay?" she asked, but before she was out of the kitchen, the telephone rang again.

"Well, I'll just bet anything that's Storm," Paige said. "Why don't you answer it?"

Sue did and it was. Paige pursed her lips and began making her spaghetti sauce.

"Sorry I missed your call, Storm," Sue told him. "I was working on my newspaper story down at Leon's Neon."

"Oh. Yeah. How's that going?"

"Well, actually, it's just beginning."

"I was wondering if you'd like to come over tonight," Storm said. "Play Scrabble or something. I'd like to see you . . . and you're the only person outside the family that Knuckles behaves for."

"Storm, I'd love to, really, but I just told Roger I'd spend the evening with him, working on the story."

"Roger *Gurney?*"

"Yes. He's the editor."

"I know."

"I'm sorry, Storm . . ."

"Me, too . . ."

"Another time?" Sue asked.

"Sure. Bye, Sue."

"Well!" Paige said when Sue had hung up. "Two dates in one night!" She smiled. "I guess you've . . . settled in, haven't you?"

Sue shook her head slowly. "I'm not sure, Aunt Paige," she answered. "I'm really not sure." But I have changed, she thought. I have begun to fit in . . . just a little . . . I have begun to be a part of other people's lives and have others a part of mine . . . just a little . . .

She gave Paige a smile that warmed her aunt's fond heart.

*

"Well, son! How was your date?" Roger Gurney Sr. boomed as Roger Jr. came through the front door.

"It wasn't exactly a date, Dad, it was more of a *working* date."

"Sure, sure," his father said. " 'Working date.' I remember those . . ."

"No, it was, Dad. We went down to Leon's. Dinah Deener was there. She took me for seventy-five cents. And there were elementary school kids there, too. At night! Spending money like you wouldn't believe!"

"And how about Frances?"

"Frances?"

"The girl you took out!"

"You mean *Sue,*" Roger said.

"Ah. Right. Her mother—her mother's name was Frances. Frances Faye Pointer. Sister was Paige . . ."

"Mrs. Stillwater."

"Yeah. I see her around every now and then . . .
Never had what her sister had . . . Frances Faye . . .
What's the daughter look like?"

"She's about five feet, brown hair—"

"Wavy?"

"Yeah, kind of . . . She has these pretty eyes—green-
ish, with long lashes . . ."

"Small nose? Slim?"

"Yeah," Roger sighed.

"Yeah," his father sighed.

*

Mrs. Hegelmeyer and Paige stood together in the
Stillwaters' back yard, beaming at young Charles Hegelmeyer who was kneeling in the grass with his arms
wrapped around his duck. Sue's eyes were on Carson, a
few paces away. She was bundled into her pink terry-
cloth bathrobe, having been wakened from sleep to say
goodbye to Marcia.

"I'm sorry we're so late," Mrs. Hegelmeyer said to
Paige. "Harry's train was delayed and then we got
lost—"

"It's all right," Paige said. "It's just that Carson went
to bed thinking you weren't coming. This is kind of a
shock for her . . ."

"I know how she feels and I am sorry. But just look
at Charlie's face!"

"Carson seems to be taking it well," Sue whispered to
Paige. "Look, she's just standing there watching Charlie, being so good . . ."

"Give her a minute," Paige whispered back. "She just
got up. She hasn't mounted her forces yet."

Charlie Hegelmeyer looked up at his mother and father and pulled a feather off his tear-stained cheek. "Look, Mom! Whitey remembers me, see?"

"Whitey!" Carson shrieked.

Paige shuddered. "Stand back," she said to Sue. "Here it comes."

"Her name is *Marcia,* not *Whitey!* Whitey is a *stupid* name!"

"Carson!" Paige cried, but it was too late. Carson reached down and grabbed the duck by the neck to pull it away from Charlie Hegelmeyer, who instinctively grabbed the neck, too, to pull the duck away from Carson.

"Charles!" Mr. Hegelmeyer called sharply and he and his wife and Paige and Sue made a dash for the children.

"Quack!" the duck screamed hoarsely as it was being yanked back and forth between Carson and Charlie.

Mr. Hegelmeyer got there first and pulled Charlie's hands away as Paige and Sue grabbed Carson.

"Carson, Carson, come on, honey, you're hurting her," Sue murmured as she comforted the little girl.

"Carson, it's Charlie's duck, darling," Paige said.

"I'm glad Whitey's getting out of here!" Charlie shrieked. "You would've killed him!"

"I would not!" Carson yelled back. "Marcia's happy here, she had a good home! *You* were the one who lost her!"

"Now, Charles," his mother said.

"Carson . . ." Paige said.

"His name's Whitey!" Charlie started toward Carson but his father held him tightly.

"It is not! It's Marcia!" Carson shrilled and Paige had to hold her, too.

Mr. Hegelmeyer picked up the duck. "Well," he said,

nodding to Paige, "it was nice meeting you. And thanks so much for . . . everything . . ."

"Whitey!"

"Marcia!"

"Nice meeting you, too," Paige answered.

"Goodnight," Mrs. Hegelmeyer said, backing toward her car.

"Whitey!"

"Marcia!"

"Night," Paige said.

"Whitey!"

"Marcia!"

"Quack!" the duck said.

— ✳ —

A week later . . .

Roger Gurney caught Sue as she was leaving her last period class and heading for her locker.

"Wait up, Sue!" he called as he pushed through the crowd toward her.

"Hi, Roger . . ."

"Hi," he panted. "I'm glad I caught you. I tracked you down through the office. I need your story now, if you've finished it."

"It's in my locker," Sue said. "I have finished it, but I thought you wanted it for the meeting tomorrow."

"I did, but I thought if it were ready, I'd go over it tonight and check it against my editorial. Is that okay?"

"Sure. My locker's at the end of the hall."

Roger took Sue's arm as they walked and Sue noticed a wink and several whispers from other students who passed them. As Storm wheeled by, she extricated her arm from Roger's and waved to him. "Hi, Storm!" she called. "See you later . . ."

Storm looked up, nodded, and wheeled on.

"Roger Gurney, what are you doing here?" Arlette trilled. "I thought all the seniors arranged their schedules so they'd have the afternoons off."

"Not everyone, Arlette. After all, there's the newspaper and besides, the astronomy course was only given last period."

They had reached Sue's locker. She opened it, took some papers off the top shelf and handed them to Roger.

"Hope it's okay, Roger," she said. "I concentrated on Dinah mostly. I'm really worried about her. I wonder if her parents know how she's caught by these games . . ."

But Roger was looking over the story.

"Mmmm, yeah. I like your lead: 'Harmless fun. The latest fad. But what's really happening to many young people as a result of the new video games playhouses springing up all over the country?' That's okay . . . Mmmmm . . . 'This reporter observed . . .' uh huh, uh huh . . . '. . . spent *ten dollars* in *forty-five minutes?*'" Roger's jaw dropped.

Sue was nodding. "She was having a bad day. The Crazy Climber dropped off the building like—that!" she snapped her fingers—"and all the balls in the pinball machine fell into holes practically as soon as she touched the flippers. Of course, she tilted . . ."

"Boy! Where'd she get all the money?"

Sue blushed. "I'm afraid, mostly from me. I'm building up a bank of tutoring sessions."

"Look, Sue," Roger said. "Let's get out of here and go get a hamburger or something. We can talk about the story."

"I'd like to, Roger, but I was due to meet Dinah in Mr. Coffee's room five minutes ago. She kept her appointment day before yesterday and I hope she keeps today's . . . I'd better get up there."

*

Mr. Coffee was alone in his room. He was seated at his desk, flipping through a pile of typewritten pages when Sue entered.

"Excuse me, Mr. Coffee," she said, "but I was hoping Dinah would be here. We were supposed to meet, remember?"

"Oh, Sue!" The teacher hastily scooped up his papers and fitted them neatly into a cardboard box.

"That looks like a large project, Mr. Coffee," Sue said.

"It is. It's—uh—my novel, my revised novel. It's, uh, it's almost finished." He grinned sheepishly at Sue as he saw her eyes widen.

"A novel! How wonderful!" Sue cried. "Can you tell me what it's about?"

"Oh, just, uh, small town living . . . you know, about living in a small town . . ."

"Sounds fascinating!"

Mr. Coffee put the lid over the box. "Well," he said, "it's a lot of hard work . . ."

"I'm sure it is," Sue said. "I never met anyone who was writing a book before . . ."

"Ah, but you're going to be published yourself very soon, aren't you, Sue? My, that's a lovely pendant you're wearing . . ." He bent closer. "What is that, a bird of some kind?"

"It's an owl. I'm afraid Dinah isn't coming. I had a feeling she wouldn't . . ."

"She's going to fail English. I know it's early in the year, but if she goes on like this—"

"I'll find her, Mr. Coffee. I'm sure she must be at Leon's. I'll go get her."

"You certainly are a good friend, Sue," Mr. Coffee called as Sue neared the door. "And conscientious and concerned and—" But Sue was gone.

*

Clutching her books and her clutch purse, Sue ran out of the school and down the street. She was so sure that Dinah would be at Leon's Neon that she would have missed seeing her coming out of the Blast Burger had Dinah not been sobbing loudly.

Sue stopped in her tracks. Dinah was with Rick and neither of them saw Sue. She could hear them clearly.

"Come on, Dinah, cut it out," Rich was saying. "Polly Platt doesn't mean anything to me . . ."

"Don't lie to me again, Rick, I just can't stand it. She said you're taking her to the football game next Saturday—"

"No, Dinah, no! You got it all wrong. *She's* taking *me!*"

"What?"

"She invited *me*, Dinah. I mean, the girl pleaded with me, how could I refuse? She wanted to go to the game, everybody has dates, she was supposed to go with Marshall Gold, but he got mononucleosis—"

"It's Homecoming, Rick! Of course everyone has dates! And you're supposed to be mine! Couldn't you just tell Polly that? I thought I was the only one you took out!"

Sue felt awkward listening as she pretended to stare at the window display of the hardware store, but she was afraid she'd lose Dinah if she went away. She could see Rick's and Dinah's reflections in the window and she watched as Rick slipped his arm around Dinah's shoulders. He mumbled something she couldn't hear.

"*Afterwards?* Meet me *afterwards?*" Dinah yelled. "What kind of date is that? Honestly, Rick, sometimes I think you just don't care about me at all!"

Then Sue saw Rick put both his hands on Dinah's

forearms and smile at her. He said something else Sue couldn't hear and then kissed Dinah lightly on the cheek. Dinah looked down at the sidewalk. Rick said something else, Dinah nodded, then Rick chucked her under the chin, smiled again and left. Sue sighed. Dinah was standing alone on the sidewalk in front of the Blast Burger, staring down at the cement.

Sue closed her eyes, took a deep breath, and turned from the hardware toward Dinah.

"Hi, Dinah!" she said cheerfully as she approached the sad little figure. Dinah didn't look up.

"Dinah, you look so thin . . ." Sue said hesitantly. She hadn't realized how gaunt the girl was until she got a good look at her in the sunlight.

Dinah pulled away. "You sound like my mother," she mumbled.

"I guess I'm going to sound like her again, because I have to tell you that I've been looking for you . . ."

"Not another After School Special with Sue Sudley!" Dinah said sharply and began to walk away.

Sue was tempted to forget it altogether, but sympathy for the girl overwhelmed her. Dinah was so alone.

"No!" She caught up with her. "I'm not letting you go. Maybe we won't do any work, but I'm going to walk you home. At least let me do that."

"Why?"

"Because you look like you could use a friend and I'm the only one around right now."

Dinah made a face but gave in. Sue trotted along beside her until they reached the Deener's house on Sycamore, four blocks from Sue's.

"Well, this is it," Dinah said. She looked toward the

driveway and saw her parents' car. She bit her lip. "You, uh, want to come in for a while?"

"Okay," Sue said. "Sure, I'd like to."

As they reached the top of the front steps, the door was yanked open by Dinah's mother.

"Well," Benita said harshly, "only an hour late today, young lady. This behavior is getting to be too much, Dinah—"

"Mother, this is—my friend. Sue Sudley."

Benita's face softened immediately. "Oh, how nice!" she said. "Paige Stillwater's niece!"

"It's nice to meet you, Mrs. Deener," Sue said.

"Well, come in, come in. Mooch! Look who's here!"

Mooch Deener appeared from the kitchen as they all stepped into the house.

"Dinah's father's working the night shift down at the terminal these days," Benita explained. "So I get to see a lot of him during the day . . ."

"Who's here?" Mooch growled. "Besides my daughter, who doesn't even remember where she lives half the time because she's out with a good-for-nothing lazy bum."

Benita coughed. "This is the Stillwaters' niece, Mooch . . ."

"Oh. Sure. Yeah. We met at the terminal the day you came in. Sally?"

"Sue."

"Right. How you getting along?"

Benita clamped her teeth together and nudged her husband in the ribs. "Isn't it nice she's Dinah's friend, Mooch?" she asked. "We've all heard what a lovely girl she is, haven't we?"

". . . Nice to meet you," Sue said.

"We're so sorry about—well, the circumstances that brought you to Palatine," Dinah's mother said, "but we're glad you're making friends . . . like our Dinah, here . . ."

"Yeah, Dinah could sure use a new friend," Mooch said. "She could also use some better school grades, a little weight on her bones and a shampoo."

"Welcome to our happy home," Dinah said, and Sue saw her smile for the first time.

"Ahhhh, she doesn't listen to anything," Mooch said and trudged back into the kitchen.

"Don't mind him," Benita whispered. "He's very upset about Dinah's behavior. We both are. I hope you'll be a nice influence on her, Sue."

Dinah glared at her mother.

"Well, I guess I'll start dinner," Benita said quickly. "Why don't you two go up to Dinah's room to talk?"

*

Dinah closed the door of her room and turned to Sue.

"Well," she said, "go ahead. Influence me."

"I guess your parents are really worried about you, Dinah," Sue said.

Dinah exhaled loudly. "Is that what it looks like?" Then: "Yeah, I guess they are. But they're no help as you can see. I'm really sorry about that, Sue. I have to put up with it but you don't."

"I don't mind. You want to do any studying? Or do you want to talk?"

Dinah sat glumly on the bed. "I'm just so crazy about Rick," she said as tears welled up in her eyes. "And when he tells me lies it messes me up so much I just want to keep playing the games because I can concentrate on them and then I don't think about Rick while I'm piling up my score . . ."

"But you could concentrate on something else instead," Sue offered. "You could read, you could study . . . And you'd be bringing up your grades while you're forgetting about Rick."

"I can't concentrate on schoolwork," Dinah said. "I never could. My mother went to junior college and all she wants is for me to go, too, and I'm just not smart enough."

Sue sat down next to her. "That's not true, Dinah. I really don't believe that, and I'll prove it to you if you give me a chance."

Dinah looked up out of the corner of her eye. "How?"

"We'll really work together. Hard. And you stay away from Leon's. After a month, if your grades aren't a lot better, I'll pay off your debts and stake you to a lost weekend there."

Dinah's eyes widened. She turned to Sue. "You'd buy me a whole weekend at Leon's Neon?"

"Uh huh. Do they give gift certificates?"

"A whole weekend? If my grades don't improve?"

"You won't get it, though, Dinah. You're going to learn. And when you do, your grades will go up. And you'll see that you're smart after all."

Dinah began to play with her fingers. "Sue?"

"What?"

"You really don't think I'm dumb?"

"No, I don't."

Dinah held out her hand. "Shake," she said. "It's a deal."

Nick poured the scotch and put it down on a bright red coaster in front of Mr. Coffee.

"How's it going, Mr. Coffee?" he asked. "How's that novel of yours?"

The teacher sipped his drink. "Okay, Nick, okay . . . it's nearly finished and I think I've got a publisher interested this time."

"Hey, no kidding!"

"Yes, but there's just something missing, some plot details I can't quite latch on to . . ."

"To make it juicier, huh?"

Mr. Coffee smiled. "Right. This publisher likes things real—uh—"

"Juicy."

"Juicy. Right."

"Well, I guess that's the stuff that sells. You'll find it, Mr. Coffee. You're a real good writer."

"Thank you, Nick, I'll drink to that!"

The door to the taproom burst open and a flustered Paige, dragging Carson by the hand, hurried in and flopped onto a stool at the extreme end of the bar.

"Hi, honey!" Nick called. "This is a nice surprise!"

Paige grunted.

"Hi, Daddy!" Carson squealed. "Can I play pinball?"

"Okay, if you don't climb up on the bar, tilt the barstool all the way back, draw on the walls of the ladies' room—"

"I know, I know, or put out the flames of the candles with my fingers after I spit on them."

"Right, baby." Nick gave her a quarter and moved down to Paige's end of the bar.

"Something wrong, Paige?" he asked. "What brings you down here?"

Paige absently picked up a pretzel from a little basket on the bar and began to break it into pieces. Nick winced as she made tiny piles with the crumbs.

"What is it, honey?" he asked again.

Paige opened her mouth, but something on the bar caught her attention. "What's this?" she asked, tracing something with her finger.

"Aw . . . I didn't want to mention it to you . . ."

"It's a 'Q'! Carved right into your beautiful new bar! A 'Q'!"

"Yeah . . ."

"Well, what's it *doing* there?"

"Aw, it was just that rowdy crowd—"

"—who's been coming into the bar at night lately, right?"

"Yeah, them, but Larchmont and I were able to handle it. We got to the guy before he carved any more. With his boy scout knife."

"A boy scout knife?"

"Makes it worse, doesn't it?"

"I'm so glad you were able to control it . . ."

"Yeah, but see, he did manage most of that 'Q.' Even the little squiggle at the bottom . . ."

"I'm really glad you have Larchmont here, Nick," Paige said. "Where is he?"

"Oh, well, you know, he's—"

"—napping. Uh huh . . ." She went back to her piles of pretzel crumbs.

"Paige, honey, you haven't told me what's on your mind and why you're pushing pretzels on the patina . . ."

"Oh, it's just . . ." Paige slapped at the bar and crumbs went flying. "Well, you know I had the propeller bronzed for Sue . . ."

"Yeah," Nick said, mopping. "That was a nice gesture. Did she find out about it yet?"

"No, I just told her I was having the burned spots cleaned off . . . Anyway, I went to get it this afternoon. It's outside in the pickup."

"Hey, you think someone'll rip it off while you're in here?"

"I really doubt it, Nick. Anyway, this is something else. I picked up the propeller and then I drove over to the luncheonette to treat Carson to a soda."

"Uh huh . . ."

"And who was having an enormous hot fudge sundae in the luncheonette but Roger Gurney, of all people!" Paige wiped her upper lip with a napkin.

"Did he upset you, Paige?"

"Oh, well, he always does, but this time it was worse. He knows Sue's here, he knows she's Frances Faye's daughter—It just seemed to trigger all that old resentment he's had toward me all these years, ever since Frances Faye left town . . ."

"He still thinks you were responsible for breaking them up?"

"Nick, there was never anything to break up. Frances Faye never cared for Roger Gurney. But he thinks our whole family conspired to keep him away from her. Just because I used to drop water bags on him from the window of the school . . ."

Nick chuckled. "Yeah, I remember," he said.

"Well, it was only because he was such a good target. Anyway, he was crushed when she left town. And this afternoon he kept asking me questions about Sue. You know, pumping me, meanly: what is she like, where did she get her writing talent, when was her birthday—"

There was a crash and Paige and Nick looked up quickly.

"Sorry," Mr. Coffee said, sliding off his stool. "I dropped my glass, Nick. But it's okay, it was empty and it didn't break—" He picked it up and put it on the bar.

"That's okay, Mr. Coffee . . . Want another?"

"No. No, Nick, thanks, I've got to go—"

"Hello, there, Joe," Paige said, forcing a smile. "I didn't see you—"

"Hello," he answered, nodding quickly. "Nice to see you—Good evening—" and he hurried to the door, bumping Carson who stuck out her tongue at his retreating back.

Nick turned back to Paige. "Now listen, honey," he said soothingly, "don't take that stuff personally. Roger Gurney always liked your sister and Sue reminds him of all that. It's nothing against you . . ."

"I'm not so sure of that, that's why I've always tried to avoid him whenever I could . . ."

"You calm down and go on home. Sue's probably wondering where you are. I'll see you later, okay?" He patted her hand.

x

Storm looked out of his living room window. He'd been waiting there since he got home from school, watching for Sue to arrive. It was almost dinner time when he saw her run quickly up the street and to the Stillwaters' front door. He sighed. It was late. She wouldn't be stopping by now. He wheeled himself over to the fireplace and was absently stroking Knuckles when the doorbell rang.

"I'll get it!" he called and wheeled to the door.

"Hi, Storm," Sue said. "Are you just starting dinner?"

He grinned at her. "No. No! Not for a while. Come on in! I just saw you running toward your house, so I figured you were late . . ."

"I thought I was, but no one was home. You don't know where Aunt Paige and Carson are, do you?"

"No. Haven't seen them since I got home. Didn't they leave a note?"

"No. At least I didn't see one. Anyway, I'm glad they're not there because it gave me a chance to come over and see you . . ."

Storm's grin widened. "Me, too. I'm glad they're not home . . ."

"I wanted to ask you something about Dinah's family."

"Oh. Like what?"

"Well, I was just there—"

"Where? At Dinah's?"

"Yes—"

"Weren't you out with Roger Gurney?"

"Roger? No, I went to Dinah's. I thought she could use a friend."

"Yeah," Storm agreed. "She can. Her parents are always on her case and the only other person she ever sees is Rick. Rick's okay, but he has a real problem with girls. He likes every one ever born."

"I made a bet with Dinah that I'll help her improve her grades in a month or I'll treat her to a whole weekend at Leon's Neon."

"You did *what*? Sue, that's crazy!"

"No, I think we can do it, but she has to cooperate. She can't cut any tutoring sessions."

"Lotsa luck," Storm said. "If you can do it, they'll put a plaque with your name on it in the Tutor's Hall of Fame."

"Dinah will do it," Sue said.

"Listen, Sue, I'm glad you came over because there's something I want to ask you."

"What?"

Storm looked at her. "Next Saturday's the Homecoming Game—"

"I heard . . ."

"We play Rackmill. They're our biggest rival."

"I know . . ."

"I would've made varsity this year . . . everyone said so . . ."

"Storm—"

"No, what I mean is, I'd like to go to the game . . . and I wouldn't at the same time . . . And I was thinking . . . that it would be so much easier for me if . . . you would go with me. If you don't already have a date. Do you? And would you?"

"I don't," Sue said, pleased. "And I would."

"Oh," Storm said. "Oh. That's great. That's just great."

As he was smiling and nodding shyly at Sue, something caught his eye at the window. He turned his wheelchair and peered out.

"Well, that's weird . . ."

"What?" Sue asked.

"Your aunt just drove up with a bronzed propeller."

— ✳ —

The Thursday before
the Homecoming Game . . .

Sue was the only one of the students filing into the school who paid any attention to Arlette. The girl was sitting on the low cement pillar at the entrance to the Palatine High path, chewing her nails and staring at her lap.

Stopping, Sue waited for Arlette to look up as everyone else trundled on past them. But Arlette didn't look up and Sue thought, how unlike Arlette not to be noticing every tiny detail with her darting little bird's eyes.

"Hi, Arlette . . ." Sue said softly so as not to startle her.

But the girl was startled. She looked at Sue, inhaled sharply and covered her mouth with her hand.

"What is it?" Sue asked.

"Hi, Sue. Nothing." The words were sharp and quick.

"Nothing?"

"Nothing." Quicker. Sharper.

"Sure?"

"Sure."

"Want to walk into school with me?" Sue asked.

"Yes—No—Later," Arlette answered.

"Uh, all right . . . See you later?"

"Later—"

Sue went on into the building, shaking her head.

Something certainly was on Arlette's mind, but what Sue wondered was why it also wasn't on the tip of Arlette's tongue at the same time, as usual.

*

When the final bell rang at two-twenty that afternoon, Sue went immediately to Mr. Coffee's room, happy to see Dinah already there and waiting for her. Dinah had been wonderful, keeping every appointment and really beginning to make progress. Sue was so excited for her that she began to break up the lessons a bit with readings from plays she loved. She had Dinah read, too, and talk about what the passages meant. Sue could tell that Dinah enjoyed it.

That afternoon, Sue was continuing work on parts of speech.

"Every one of the boys are going to the party," Dinah recited, chewing her pencil.

"No, Dinah, now think about what we said . . ." Sue cautioned.

"Every one of the boys *were*—"

"Uh-uh-uh . . ."

"Every one . . ."

"Now leave out 'of the boys' and try it . . ."

"Every one . . . *was!*" Dinah cried happily. "Every one of the boys *was* going to the party!"

"Right!" Sue said and clapped her hands together. "Now tell me why."

"Because it was a good party?" Dinah asked.

"No, no, Dinah, why did you use *was* instead of *were?*"

"Oh! Because 'every one' is singular, not plural!"

"Terrific, Dinah. Aren't you proud?"

Dinah smiled. "Yeah," she breathed. "I'm getting it,

aren't I, Sue? You know, yesterday I didn't go into Leon's Neon once?"

"Really?"

"Really. I walked by it a few times and I nearly went in, but I didn't. I'm not borrowing any more money, and I'm trying to pay back what I already owe. Sue . . . could we read that neat speech again? The one we read yesterday from Shakespeare? I forget which play it was . . ."

"I know the one you mean," Sue said, opening a thick book. "I have it marked: page 789. Jaques' speech from *As You Like It.*

> 'All the world's a stage,
> And all the men and women merely players.
> They have their exits and their entrances,
> And one man in his time plays many parts—' "

"That's the one," Dinah said. "I like that. I like to think of everyone being actors in a big play. Because if life is just a big play, then somehow it makes you think it all will probably come out happy, because the playwright can just fix up the things that go wrong."

"Uh, well, but Dinah—"

"Oh, it's okay, Sue, I know there's no playwright writing my life, but somehow, when I think of everyone I know just acting out parts it makes me laugh more, instead of cry. Go on, read the rest of it."

"Sure.

> 'And one man in his time plays many parts,
> His acts being seven ages. At first the infant,
> Mewling and puking in the nurse's arms—' "

"Blagh!" The sound came from the supply closet. Both Sue and Dinah looked up sharply.

"What was that?" Dinah asked, and both girls got up, as the closet door opened widely and Arlette came out.

"What are you doing in there, Arlette?" Dinah asked.

"Were you there all the time?" Sue asked.

"Don't worry, I wasn't eavesdropping on you, I was getting supplies," Arlette said. "I only heard that last part because I was finished and ready to leave."

"We've been here a half-an-hour, Arlette. How long does it take you to get supplies, anyway?" Dinah demanded. "You just wanted to hear my lesson so you could go out and tell Rick how dumb I am. You call yourself a friend, Arlette—"

"No, really, Dinah—I wasn't." Arlette looked very pale and Dinah stopped haranguing her. "Honest, I wasn't listening to you, I was—Look, Dinah, I need to talk to Sue right away. And it's private, okay, Dinah?"

Sue shook her head. "It has to wait, Arlette, I'm sorry. Dinah and I aren't through yet."

"It can't wait, Sue. Look, Dinah—" Arlette opened her purse and took out her wallet. "Here's four dollars. It's all I've got, but you can play sixteen games—"

"No! Arlette!" Sue cried. "Don't give her that money. Don't you know she's quit the games?"

"Cold turkey?" Arlette asked. "Wow . . ."

But Dinah was reaching for the money. "But she's giving it to me, Sue . . . I don't have to pay it back . . ."

"Dinah, don't!"

"Just this once, Sue, just this once," Dinah was blubbering. "I promise I won't start again, but just this once, free money . . ." She looked quickly at Sue, then grabbed the bills from Arlette's hand and dashed from the room.

Sue glowered at Arlette.

"Do you know what you've done, Arlette?" she said angrily. "She was doing so well—"

"Sue, I'm sorry, I'm so sorry, but I had to talk to you and it couldn't wait."

Arlette was turning so pale Sue was afraid she'd fade away.

"Okay, sit down, Arlette. I'll try to grab Dinah after you tell me what's so important."

They sat at two desks across from each other.

"I've been in the supply closet for three days," Arlette began.

"*What?*"

"No, I don't mean I *lived* there, but I kept going back any free time I had, whenever Mr. Coffee wasn't here. Lunch time, study hall, after school, *before* school—"

"*Why?*"

"Well, originally I went in to get some typing paper. To type up my story for *The Palatine Prattler*. So I opened up this big box of typing paper and there was typing paper in it all right, but it wasn't blank. See, what was in this box was a carbon copy."

"A carbon copy of what?"

"Of a book. *This Time of Passion.*"

"*This Time of Passion?*"

"That's the title, Sue. But he's not kidding. What a book!"

"*Who's* not kidding, Arlette?" Sue was getting impatient.

"Mr. Coffee. It's his book. *This Time of Passion* by Joseph LeMay Coffee. It's on the title page. And three-quarters of it is about you."

"*Me?*"

"Yes. I know it wasn't right for me to read it, but it's not as if I deliberately sneaked in to spy or anything. I mean, there it was, all of it, in a box that was supposed to contain typing paper in the *supply closet,* which is certainly available to every—"

"Arlette, what do you mean, it's about *me?*" Sue interrupted.

"About you and your family. Your aunt and your mother . . . See it's about this small town, a town just like Palatine, and in this book there's a doctor whose wife runs away with the owner of a hangout—"

"Like Mr. Coffee's wife did?"

"Just like that only the guy was a doctor. And then it tells about this neighborhood bar—"

"Uncle Nick's."

"Yeah, and a sexy cheerleader—"

"Bonnie."

"Right. And a kid who's on the make for every girl in town—"

"Rick?"

"Uh huh. And then it tells about this big business executive, he's president of some corporation, and when he was young he was in love with this local girl and they had a thing or something and her family found out and apparently she was pregnant and they got her out of town and she never came back . . ."

"Oh!" Sue squeaked and covered her mouth with her hand.

". . . and the next thing the executive knew, the girl—

well, she was a woman then—was killed in an airplane crash with her husband and after the crash the girl's daughter, who was really this executive's daughter, are you following me? came back to live in this town where her mother had grown up. Came back to live with her mother's sister."

Sue was sitting in the same position with her hand over her mouth.

"Sue?" Arlette said. "Well, you see, Sue, why I had to talk to you?"

Sue didn't move.

"Sue? Oh, Sue, say something, Sue, speak, Sue—"

A gurgle came from Sue's throat.

"Take deep breaths," Arlette said. "Put your head between your legs. That's it. Now breathe . . . breathe . . . breathe . . . Feel better?"

Sue sat up dizzily. "Where's Mr. Coffee, Arlette, do you know?"

"As a matter of fact, I do know. I overheard him telling the principal. He's leaving town. He's going to Cincinnati to have lunch tomorrow with the publisher who's interested in his book. He took the original with him and left the copy here."

". . . in the supply closet . . ."

"In the supply closet. I would have told you sooner but I had to finish the book first."

"Is it going to be published?" Sue asked weakly.

"Well, I guess publishers don't invite you to Cincinnati to have lunch unless they're serious. This is a hot book, Sue, I mean, there are chapters about this business executive and the sexy cheerleader and—"

"Arlette, please—"

"Sorry."

"Look, Arlette, I know this is going to be the hardest thing you've ever done in your life, but please, *please* don't tell anyone about this . . ."

Arlette gasped. "Honestly, Sue! How can you even suggest that I would! Didn't I even *bribe* Dinah to leave us alone? I wouldn't breathe a *word*, Sue, really!"

"Thank you, Arlette." Sue stood up and steadied herself. "I've got to get home and tell Aunt Paige. She'll know what to do. You are sure about all this, aren't you?"

"It's right in there if you want to see for yourself."

"I don't, I believe you . . ."

Sighing heavily, Arlette sank back into her chair and watched Sue stumble shakily out of the room.

*

Mooch Deener smacked the top of his desk in disgust, sending papers, old lunch bags, candy wrappers and schedules flying off in all directions. He had forgotten the bag of sandwiches and snacks Benita always packed for him in the evenings when he went to work. The night dispatcher's job wasn't often very demanding and he had a lot of time to himself. He liked to spend that time eating and reading mystery novels. The novels were there but without the food they didn't seem as appealing and he grumbled out loud and slapped at the desk again.

"What's wrong, Mooch? Overworked, here at our thriving metropolis? Too many vehicles to keep track of? Not enough assistance or equipment? Never any—"

"Okay, okay, enough," Mooch said with a grin to Mr. Coffee, who was leaning over the sill of his window. "Naw, Joe, I just forgot my eats for tonight, that's all.

Benita makes great snacks—they get me through. You meeting someone or leaving?"

"Leaving, Mooch, I'm leaving. Just for overnight, though. I'll be back tomorrow evening."

Mooch looked at his watch. "You'd be catching the bus for Cinci, then, eh?"

"Uh huh. Have an important lunch date. I think I'll have some exciting news when I come back."

"Oh, yeah? What's that?"

"Tell you tomorrow, if things work out . . ."

"Well, I guess you'd be back tomorrow all right. Wouldn't want to miss the big game, would you?"

"Homecoming? Not on your life. I'll be there. Where's the bus, Mooch?"

"It's out there, Joe. You can't miss it. It's big and grey with red lettering, it says 'Cincinnati' up front and it's also the only one out there. It's almost ready to go."

"Thanks, Mooch. Oh, hello, Benita."

Benita Deener had come into the terminal, carrying a large brown bag. She smiled at the English teacher and waved as he went out to board his bus.

"Hey! Swell! Thanks, Benita! The night's looking up after all," Mooch said, taking the bag through his window. "I didn't want to call you, drag you down here and all . . ."

"It's okay, Mooch. I made the stuff, I didn't want it to go to waste. I knew you'd be mad to have forgotten it."

"Yeah, I was."

"Where's Joe going?"

"Cinci. Overnight. Said he'd have some news when he came back. Want a bite of this?"

"Yuck! No. Only you can eat pickles and herring. What news?"

"Didn't say. Where's Dinah?"

"Not home yet. I hope she's okay. You know how good she's been lately about coming right home and studying . . ."

Mooch smiled. "Yeah. She seems to have turned over a new leaf. Wonder if she's still seeing that Rick on the sly."

Benita shook her head. "I don't know," she said. "He used to be all she'd talk about, but she hasn't mentioned him much lately. Of course, that doesn't mean anything . . . Oh, there goes the Cincinnati bus pulling out . . . How long will Joe be gone? He'll be back by Saturday, won't he?"

"I asked him, he said sure. He wouldn't miss the Homecoming Game."

"Do we stand a chance of beating Rackmill this year?"

"I don't know, Benita. I wish Storm could play. This'd be his first year on the varsity squad, but that kid was better on j.v. than most of the older boys on varsity now . . ."

"I know." She leaned heavily on the sill. "Busy tonight?"

"Toledo's due in any minute now." Mooch looked at his watch. "Any minute," he repeated. "In fact . . ." He looked up. "Here it is now."

Benita looked around the waiting room. An old man was asleep on one of the benches and a teenage boy was buying candy from a vending machine.

"I guess nobody's waiting for it," she said.

"Want to guess how many people get off? I'll bet you a movie it's . . ."

"Five?" Benita said quickly.

"Never," Mooch said. "You lose. I bet two."

"Only two?"

"It's a Thursday night, Benita. On Sunday we could have as many as six."

"Well, let's see . . ."

They both craned their necks toward the door.

"If I lose will you still take me to a movie?" Benita asked.

And just as Mooch was about to say "Sure," they both dropped their jaws at the sight of the one passenger stepping into the terminal from the incoming Toledo bus.

"Lord!" Benita whispered hoarsely. "Will you look who it is!"

"Joanna Coffee!" Mooch whispered back. "Isn't it?"

"It sure is!" Benita stepped away from the window and planted herself almost directly in the younger woman's path, but Joanna Coffee kept walking toward the outside door.

"Well!" Benita said huffily. "Not even a 'hello'!"

"She didn't even see you, Benita," Mooch said. "Or me, either."

"Of course she saw me! She's probably too embarrassed to face me, that's all! Running off like she did. It's a wonder she's showing her face back here again."

"Funny thing is she just missed Joe!" Mooch remembered. "He goes and she comes! Isn't that strange, Benita?"

But Benita was lost in thought. "Joanna Coffee," she mumbled softly. "Back in town. And alone, too. I wonder what happened between her and Leon?"

*

"*What?*" Paige screamed and Carson jumped, spilling her glass of milk.

"I told you," Sue said in her softest voice. She was still shaken. "Mr. Coffee's written a novel and it seems to be about us . . ."

"The crash?"

"Yes . . ."

"And Frances Faye and Roger Gurney?"

"Who?"

"Never mind. Who did the young local girl have an affair with? In the book, I mean?"

"Arlette said it was a business executive. Aunt Paige, did *Mother*—?"

"No! Of course she didn't. Are you absolutely positively surely *sure* about this, Sue?"

"Yes, Aunt Paige, Arlette told me she'd read the whole thing!"

"Ohh!" Paige slapped one hand against her forehead and the other against her chest. "Coffee! How could he? Where did he *get* such stuff—"

"Well, some . . . from my essay . . ." Sue said, "about the—about what happened last summer . . . I told you about that . . ."

"Did you write anything about your mother's background? About her leaving Palatine and everything?"

"No! No, I didn't!"

Paige began to pace. "The bar. A week. Ten days ago. Two weeks . . ."

"What?" Sue asked.

"The bar. Joe Coffee was in the bar. After I ran into . . . The day I had your propeller bronzed . . ."

"That was such a lovely thing to do," Sue said.

"I talked to Nick. He heard me . . . He made up the part about—Oh, Lord . . . I have to find him right away."

"You can't. I already thought about that. He's in Cincinnati, talking to a publisher."

"A publisher? You mean a *real* publisher?"

"Arlette said she overheard him telling the principal."

Paige wiped her brow. "Sue, have you ever known Arlette to be *wrong* in all this gossip she spreads?"

"No."

"Neither have I. What are we going to *do?*"

"I don't know," Sue said. "I wish I did."

*

Bunny Ryder was just leaving Palatine's Parties-Presents-Prescriptions Drug Store with some aspirin and two bottles of Pepto Bismol when she saw what looked exactly like Joanna Coffee walking toward her down the street. When Bunny realized that yes, it actually was Joanna Coffee, she dropped her paper bag, breaking the bottles of Pepto Bismol and leaving a spreading pink blob on the sidewalk at her feet. Bunny walked right through it.

"Joanna?" she said to the young woman, who did not even turn to look at her. "Joanna?" Bunny said again, louder.

The woman turned slowly.

"Joanna, it is you, isn't it? Don't you know me?"

The woman shook her head.

"It's me, Joanna. Bunny! Bunny Ryder!"

But the woman didn't answer.

"When did you come back, Joanna?" Bunny asked, touching her arm. What on earth is wrong with her,

Bunny thought. She looks like she's in an absolute daze!

"Who's Jo—Joanna?"

Bunny muttered, "Oh, boy," under her breath and aloud said, "Don't you know your name, Joanna?"

"No," the woman answered. "I don't know my name . . ."

"This is your town, Joanna. You must have known that . . . You came back. You've been away and you came back. So you know where you are, don't you?" Bunny kept trying to look Joanna Coffee in the eye but the woman didn't seem to be focusing.

"No . . . I don't know where I am exactly . . . But I always come home for Homecoming . . ."

Bunny inhaled. She's home for Homecoming, she thought. If that isn't the living end!

"Look, Joanna, does Joe know you're here?"

"Joe?"

"Your husband. Joe. Joe Coffee. Don't you remember?"

"No . . ."

Oh, good grief, Bunny thought. "Well, where are you going? Right now, I mean. You've got a suitcase . . . Did you just get back in town?"

"I got off a bus . . ."

"From where, Joanna?"

"I don't remember."

"Do you know where you're going right now?" Bunny asked again, though she was pretty sure of the answer.

"No . . ."

"Thought so. Listen, Joanna, why don't you come with me? I'm on my way home—to my own house— and I'll take you there and we'll call Joe, okay?"

"I don't know a Joe," Joanna mumbled as Bunny

steered her toward her car, trailing sticky pink footprints on the sidewalk behind her.

*

Will Ryder, Storm's father, rushed to quiet Knuckles, who had begun to bark furiously as soon as he heard the car door close outside.

"Quiet, Knuckles!" Storm called, and his father said, "Come on, Knuckles, it's only Mother, it's only Mother, boy . . ."

But when the door opened they saw it wasn't only Mother.

"Mrs. Coffee!" Storm gasped.

"Joanna?" Will said.

"She doesn't know," Bunny explained.

"Doesn't know what?"

"Doesn't know who she is. Will, take her suitcase and let's get her over to the couch," Bunny directed.

Storm took Joanna's raincoat and Bunny settled her on the couch, while Will put the suitcase next to the wall near the front door.

"I'm going to make you some tea, dear," Bunny said to Joanna who was busy looking from face to face. "All right?"

"She looks like she could use a drink," Will said out of the side of his mouth.

"Would you rather have a drink, Joanna?"

"I don't know," Joanna answered.

Bunny nodded at Will. "Tea, I think," she said and went off into the kitchen with Storm wheeling after her.

"Joanna," Will Ryder said, sitting down next to her on the couch, "where's Leon?"

"Who's Leon?" Joanna asked blankly.

"Oh, boy," Will said, rolling his eyes. "Bunny?" he called toward the kitchen. "Does Joe know she's here?"

"No!" his wife called back. "Phone him, will you?"

"Okay!"

When Bunny came in with the hot tea, her husband was hanging up the phone and shaking his head.

"I let it ring maybe twenty times," Will said.

"No answer?"

"No. Where do you think he'd be? Stillwater's?"

"I don't know. He could be anywhere. Storm, was Mr. Coffee in school today? Drink your tea, dear . . ."

"Yeah," Storm said, nodding. "He was there. Oh, but he did say we'd have a substitute tomorrow, though. He gave us a special assignment."

"Hmmmmm . . ." Bunny mused. "Did he say he'd be out all day or just for your class?"

"He didn't say. But Sue's in a different English class with him. Maybe she'd know something. Should I call her?"

"Yes, sure," Bunny said. "Try her, try anything."

Storm dialed and heard a distraught-sounding Sue answer his greeting.

"What's wrong, Sue?" he asked, concerned. "You sound awful!"

He listened a moment, then turned to his mother. "She says it is awful and it's a long story and it has to do with Mr. Coffee."

"Mr. Coffee!" Bunny cried. "Storm, give me that phone." She took the receiver from him and began to talk. "Sue, dear, this is Mrs. Ryder, I've got to speak to your Aunt Paige right away. I've got Mr. Coffee's wife right here with me now and she's got amnesia!"

— ✳ —

Saturday, the day of the Homecoming Game . . .

The first thing Storm noticed when Sue answered the door was the darkness under her eyes, and the deeper hollows in her cheeks.

She tried to smile at him. "Hi, Storm," she said.

"You sure you still want to go?" he asked tentatively. "You look like—well, kind of like you didn't get much sleep last night. I missed you in school yesterday . . ."

"We all stayed home yesterday," Sue sighed. "But you're right . . . we haven't gotten much sleep since Thursday. Anyway, of course I'll still go to the game with you, Storm. Do you want to come in for a minute?"

"Sure." Storm wheeled himself into the Stillwaters' living room and Sue sat down on a footstool next to him.

"How's Mrs. Coffee this morning?" Sue asked.

"The same. She slept all day yesterday and she was still sleeping when I left. Boy, Sue, she didn't know *any* of us. It was really spooky."

"I can imagine . . ."

"But she's going to the game. Would you believe it? That's why she came home. For Homecoming. It's all she remembers."

Paige, in a purple chenille bathrobe, stumbled into the room.

"Oh, hello, Storm," she said absently. "I nearly forgot about today . . . I guess you're here to pick up Sue . . ."

"Yes, Ma'am—"

"Sue, you're going to look for Joe Coffee, aren't you? Bunny said Benita said Mooch said he's coming back today and will probably be at the game." Paige brushed a lock of hair out of her eyes and sat on the couch. "I should probably go, too, but I just can't face the crowd . . . Nick's getting the bar all ready for afterwards . . . Oh, Sue, what if you see him? What will you say?"

"Don't worry, Aunt Paige," Sue told her. "I don't know what I'll say, but I'll find out something. If he's there . . ."

"If he's there . . ." Paige repeated.

"Sue's not the only one Mr. Coffee'll have to face at the game," Storm said. "Mrs. Coffee's going to be there, too."

"Oh, good Lord," Paige muttered. "That Joe Coffee, I could just kill him, him and his poetic license!"

Sue stood up. "Aunt Paige, why don't you just try and get some sleep? Storm and I will leave now. That should give us plenty of time to get there and still be early."

"All right, dear . . . but I don't think I'll be able to sleep. Maybe I'll go over and see Joanna before she leaves for the game . . ."

*

Bunny Ryder balanced the breakfast tray with one hand while she knocked softly on the guest room door with the other.

"Joanna?" she called.

A faint voice answered, "Yes? Come in . . ."

Bunny had expected to find Joanna in bed where she'd spent all day Friday, hardly speaking or eating. But there she was, dressed in her clothes from Thursday night, combing her hair in front of the little vanity mirror.

"I brought you some breakfast, Joanna," Bunny said, putting the tray down on a night table. "How are you feeling this morning?"

"Oh, all right, thank you, uh—"

"Bunny. Bunny Ryder. I told you yesterday. And the day before."

"Bunny . . . Thank you, but I really don't feel very hungry . . . Is it time for the game?"

"No, dear, you have plenty of time. Are you sure you want to go? Why is it so important you go to the game, Joanna?"

"I never miss a Homecoming . . . I must go . . ."

"I see . . . Joe will be there, I understand . . . Joanna?"

"Joe who?"

Bunny sighed. "Never mind," she said, as Will called to her from the living room.

"Paige is here, Bunny!" he yelled.

"Oh! Joanna, it's Paige. Paige Stillwater. Remember? Up here, Paige! The guest room!"

Joanna continued to comb her hair. Bunny tiptoed out into the hall and met Paige at the top of the stairs.

"She won't know you," Bunny whispered. "She doesn't even remember Joe. She's getting ready for the game."

"Are you going with her?" Paige asked.

"No, I made a beauty parlor appointment for today. I can't go to the games now that Storm's—"

"I understand."

"Will might go, though. Anyway, I don't think it would matter one way or another to Joanna . . ." Bunny took Paige's arm and led her into the guest room.

"Hi, Joanna," Paige said. "Golly, you look . . . wonderful."

"Thank you . . . is it time to go now?"

Paige looked at Bunny and Bunny looked at Paige.

*

Storm put his hands down to stop the chair from wheeling further.

"What is it, Storm?" Sue asked from behind the chair.

"Listen . . ."

"To what?"

"They're warming up . . ."

From the field they heard the players counting out their exercises.

"Jumping jacks . . ." Storm whispered.

It sounded to Sue like husky foghorns.

"Whun-two-three-fuh-"

"Do you want to wait here?" Sue asked.

"No . . . let's go get our seats. Then I won't be in the way when the crowd arrives."

"Okay . . ."

The cheerleaders were practicing near the benches. Bonnie broke away from them when she saw Storm and Sue and rushed over to them.

"Come on, Storm, you come right down here to the

127

team bench," she said, taking the chair from Sue. "We all want you right there near the action."

"Bonnie," Storm began, "it's not necessary to—"

"No, everyone wants you there, Storm. You, too, Sue, you can stay right with him. It's all right. Storm's special."

Storm smiled. "Thanks, Bonnie. Hey, that's some . . . uniform."

Bonnie wiggled. "Yeah, it is, isn't it. It was my idea to have lowcut sweaters. And look where we sewed the megaphones."

"I am looking . . ."

The team began to do pushups. As each player noticed Storm, he called and waved at him. Storm nodded, smiled and waved back.

"Are you okay, Storm?" Sue whispered over his shoulder.

"Yeah, I'm okay," he answered, but she wasn't so sure. He had a funny look in his eye.

As people began to arrive and fill up the bleachers, Sue craned her neck for a glimpse of Mr. Coffee, but all the students filing down to the team bench to say hello to Storm blocked her view. Arlette tapped her on the shoulder and she turned quickly, startled.

"Oh! Arlette, I'm glad to see you," Sue said. "With everything that's happened I haven't had a chance to catch up with Dinah. As a matter of fact, I haven't seen her at all since Thursday. Do you know how she is? Or where she is?"

"No, I haven't seen her either," Arlette said. "She's not here yet and Rick is here with Polly Platt. Mr. Coffee isn't here either, but he will be. I'll bet you're just dying to see *him*. I heard all about Mrs. Coffee coming back but not a soul knows anything about Leon. The principal's in a fury about the new cheerleading uniforms and—"

"Arlette, please, I don't have time to listen to your column now, I'm trying to find Mr. Coffee or Di—"

"I'm not reading, Sue, I'm *talking!*"

"Oh."

Suddenly, Arlette squealed. "There she is, there's Mrs. Coffee!" she cried, pinching Sue's arm.

"Where?"

"Up there. In the center of the third row. See? She's wearing a yellow raincoat."

"Is Mr. Coffee with her?"

"No . . . I don't see him. I wonder if he made it back after all . . ."

Storm spent all the time before the kickoff greeting his friends and Sue spent it looking for Mr. Coffee and Dinah. She was so absorbed she missed the kickoff. The drone of the cheerleaders made her turn around.

"Pal-a-tine, Pal-a-tine, have no fear! Rack-mill, Rackmill, in your EAR!" Sue looked at Storm as the crowd chanted, "Whoa-oa-oa-oa-oa-*OH!*" back at the cheerleaders and saw that he was slightly paler.

Out on the field, the Rackmill quarterback was running toward the sidelines, looking for a receiver.

"*Cream 'im!*" Storm yelled, but the quarterback ran out of bounds. "Ahhh, Koblenski!" Storm screamed at Palatine's defensive tackle.

Sue leaned over. "Storm?" she said, but he ignored her. "Storm, I can't find Mr. Coffee at all. And I don't see Dinah, either. I'm so afraid she may have suffered a relapse . . . What do you think?"

But Storm stared straight ahead with glassy eyes. Sue

kept trying, but it was as though she weren't even there. Storm was riveted to the action on the field and would occasionally groan or mumble something Sue didn't understand. After a while, she lost track of the game, trying to pull Storm out of his trance and trying to make out the faces of the people above her in the stands.

"GO-O-O-O-O-O-OH, PAL-A-TINE!" Bonnie's cheerleaders yelled at the end of a play, but Sue was hardly aware of them, and at halftime she couldn't have told a soul that the score was 6-0, in favor of Rackmill High.

Over the loudspeaker a nasal voice was crying, "Ladies and gentlemen, will you please welcome: the famous, the fabulous, the fabled *Palatine High School Marching Band!*"

"Storm," Sue said over the din. "Storm, would you like a soda? Or something?"

Storm stared straight ahead.

"Storm, they're selling food over there. Can I get you something?" Sue repeated, but Storm didn't answer her.

"Storm, I'm going to look for Mr. Coffee, okay? Okay, Storm?" When he still didn't respond, Sue said, "It's okay, Storm, I'll leave you alone for a minute if that's what you want. I'll be back for the start of the second half . . ."

*

Mr. Coffee had arrived after the opening kickoff and instead of fighting his way through the bleachers, decided to stand at the end of them and watch from there, out of the way. As the famous, fabulous and fabled Palatine Marching Band strutted out onto the field playing

Mountain Greenery, he realized he was hungry and began to push through to the food wagon.

*

"Can I get you something, Joanna?" Will Ryder asked.

Joanna Coffee put her finger up to her lips thoughtfully. "There was something I came for . . ." she mumbled, "but I don't remember. It's Homecoming, isn't it?"

"Yes . . . this is the Rackmill game."

"Rackmill and—?"

"Palatine."

"Yes . . ."

"Would you like something to eat?" he asked again.

"All right . . . No, no thanks . . . Well, maybe . . ."

She got up before he could stop her and began to work her way across the row. He stood, then, and looked down at the team bench, where Storm was bent over in his wheelchair, his head resting on his fist.

Will's heart went out to his boy. Sue was nowhere to be seen, so he decided to spend halftime with Storm. As he stepped over the bleacher below, he saw Joe Coffee cross ahead of him on the grass. Will forgot Storm momentarily as he realized that the English teacher would probably meet Joanna at the food line!

"Joe!" he cried as loudly as he could, but Mr. Coffee didn't turn around. Will pressed forward, mumbling to himself. "I've got to get him before he sees her that way . . . What a way to meet . . . oh, Lord—Joe! Joe!" He leaped back up on a bench to get a better vantage point. Sure enough, there was Joanna, but—but—

*

"Hel-lo, Mrs. Coffee!"

"Hm?"

"It's me, Arlette Levine. You know me. It's nice to have you back in town!" Arlette chirped. "Are you getting some food? A drink? Some coffee, Mrs. Coffee? Can I get it for you?"

Joanna stared at Arlette.

"Mrs. Coffee?"

"I'm home for Homecoming," Joanna said to Arlette and then turned away toward the front gates.

Arlette repeated, "Mrs. Coffee?" several times, but Joanna had moved on through the crowd. And then Arlette spotted Joe. Jumping up and down and waving the orange pompom Bonnie had lent her, she began to call. "Mr. Coffee! Mr. Coffee! Over here, over here!"

"Hey, leave the guy alone, Arlette," someone at her elbow said. "Don't you pester him enough in school?"

"Oh, it's you, Rick," Arlette said, turning around. Rick was balancing two hot dogs and two sodas. "Those aren't for Dinah, are they?"

"Maybe," Rick answered. "They're not for you, anyway."

"I know who they're for, Polly Platt, you rat. And oh, now you made me lose him!"

"You never had him, Arlette." Rick laughed as he moved away. "Oh, hi, Mr. Ryder."

"Hello, Rick," Will Ryder said, as he looked over the boy's head. "You haven't seen Joe Coffee around here, have you? I thought he was heading for the food . . ."

"Well, yeah, I did, a second ago, but—oh, hey, there goes the team back on the field. Second half, Mr. Ryder. See ya!"

"Yeah . . . See ya, Rick . . ."

*

Sue knelt down next to Storm's chair.

"I'm sorry, Storm," she said. "There was such a crush I never did get to the food wagon. Are you okay?"

"Uh . . ." Storm said.

"Storm, I'm getting worried about you," Sue said, but Storm just muttered, "Go. Kick. Pillage. Destroy." And Sue sighed.

*

The seat next to Will Ryder remained empty as the second half began and he scanned the crowd in vain for Joanna Coffee. Sipping his grape soda he mumbled, "Bunny will kill me," but as soon as Rackmill kicked off, he forgot about her.

*

Joanna wandered past Stillwater's Taproom, past the Little Fellers Pet Shop, past the Post Office, past the store with the cool aviator jackets that had so impressed Rick. The streets of Palatine were empty. She stopped suddenly when she reached a building with two small wooden doors. Turning purposefully she opened them and stepped inside, blinking as the lights flashed and swirled about her. Weaving slightly, she looked around.

Melissa, the changegirl, leaned against the wall, jingling the change in her apron and cracking her gum. Once in a while she'd glance over at the only customer in the place—a skinny blonde, working fitfully at City-Lights Pinball.

"You're gonna tilt it, Dinah," Melissa drawled, but the girl pushed the machine again.

"I'm tellin' you," the changegirl warned again.

Bzzzzzz-zzz-zz-z went the machine.

"I told you," Melissa yawned.

Dinah gave the machine a savage kick, whirled quickly and sat on the floor, covering her face with her hands.

"You want something?" Melissa said to Joanna, and then: "That you, Mrs. Coffee?"

Dinah looked up. Joanna was staring straight ahead.

"Mrs. Coffee?" the changegirl said again and walked toward her.

Dinah got up off the floor and followed Melissa, who was now peering into Joanna's face.

"Mrs. Coffee," Dinah said, "what are you doing here?"

"Hello," Joanna said.

"It's me. Dinah. Dinah Deener. See?"

"Hello," Joanna said.

Dinah looked at the changegirl, who shrugged.

"Are you sick, Mrs. Coffee?" Dinah asked.

"I came home," Joanna said. "For Homecoming."

"Uh huh . . ." Dinah said. "What about Le—" she began, and stopped.

"I think I know this place," Joanna said. "At least I thought I did when I came in, but now I'm not so sure . . ."

"You're not sure you know this place?" Dinah repeated. "Do you know me? Do you know Melissa here?"

Joanna didn't answer.

"Where's Leon?" Melissa asked. Dinah stuck an elbow in Melissa's ribs, but Joanna didn't respond to the question at all.

"She must have amnesia," Melissa hissed. "She doesn't remember anything."

Dinah made a face. "Well, she's not deaf, Melissa. She

can *hear* you." She took Joanna's arm and led her past Melissa over to a bench against the wall. "Come on," she said. "Sit down here. Can you tell me where you're staying?"

"Staying?"

"Are you back at your apartment?"

"Apartment?"

"Over on Richman. With Mr. Coffee. Joe. Mr. Coffee. Your husband."

"Husband?"

Dinah said "Yikes" under her breath.

"Hey, Dinah?" Melissa called. "You've still got fifty cents coming for that two hours you worked for me yesterday . . . You gonna play anymore? Because if you're not, I think I'll close up . . . Nobody's comin' in anyway, I bet, and I can go catch the rest of the game."

Dinah didn't answer, but rubbed her eyes. What should I do with her, she thought. She's worse off than *I* am! I thought I was walking around in a daze . . .

"Dinah?"

"No, close up, Melissa. Do whatever you want. I'm going to try to do something for Mrs. Coffee. I don't know what yet, but if everybody's at the game then I'm the only one around who can help for now. I guess I'll have to think of the best place to take her . . ."

✳

By the fourth quarter, Palatine had scored a touchdown, but missed the extra point. The game was tied, 6-6.

Palatine had Rackmill back on their own 30-yard-line. On first down, Rackmill ran a halfback draw and Palatine stopped them for no-gain. Now it was second-and-ten. The whole bench was screaming "Hold 'em! Hold 'em!" and Bonnie's pompoms were bouncing crazily back and forth. Rackmill lined up in a standard T-formation but suddenly shifted into the "I" and sent their fullback straight up the middle. It looked like a big gainer, but the defensive tackle shot a hand out and tripped up the big fullback just as he hit the line.

Now it was third-and-nine.

"Pal-a-tine, you're do-ing fine! Hold 'em! Hold 'em! Hold—that—*line!*" the cheerleaders screamed.

"Watch out for the pass!" the coach yelled.

"No," Storm mumbled. Only Sue heard him. "No. No. They're not going to pass. They're setting us up for an end-around . . ."

"What?" Sue said, leaning forward.

Sure enough, as the speedy Rackmill right end came tearing toward midfield, the crowd rose to its feet to see a day-glo orange wheelchair cut diagonally across the field to intercept the ball carrier.

*

The ambulance's siren screamed its warning through the streets of Palatine, though there didn't seem to be a soul moving, in either the business or residential areas.

Storm lay on the gurney inside the ambulance, with Sue at his feet and Will at his head. Storm's eyes were closed but his lips moved continuously and occasionally his garbled words were audible and clear.

"Motrim!" Storm suddenly yelled.

"What's 'motrim'?" Sue whispered to the attendant who shrugged.

"Arnie Motrim," Will answered. "He's Palatine's defensive halfback."

"Oh," Sue said. She reached for Storm's hand, limply hanging over the edge of the gurney. "It's all right, Storm," she murmured, "everything's going to be all right . . ."

"It's okay, boy," Will echoed. "I'm here. Your dad's here. Everything's going to be all right . . ."

"The Rackmill tight end fumbles!" Storm suddenly bellowed in his delirium.

"Shhh," Sue quieted him. "Hush, Storm . . ."

"He *fumbles!*" Storm said again. "The ball's bouncing around—"

"Storm, boy . . ." Will whispered.

"Grab it! Come on, grab it!" Storm yelled. "AH!"

Will leaned down toward Storm's mouth. "What happened?" he whispered.

"Rackmill's got it!" Storm cried.

"Ah!" Will breathed.

"No! No, they missed it! *We've* got it!"

"Yeah?" from Will.

"No, *we* missed it, *they've* got it!"

Will slapped his fist into his palm.

"No! *They* missed it! *We've* got it again!"

"Hold it! Hold it!" Will cried and inhaled sheepishly as Sue frowned at him.

"Motrim scoops up the ball, he turns on the afterburners, he sprints (mumble)—"

Will leaned down again. "What?" he said in spite of himself. "Motrim sprints—what, Storm?"

"Motrim . . . (mumble)"

"What?" the ambulance attendant cried.

". . . forty-five yards into the end zone!" Storm yelled. "The crowd's going wild!"

"Yay!" cried the attendant, and Sue said, "We're here."

"What?" Will asked.

"We're here. At the hospital."

*

A nurse's starched whites began to wilt as she tried to push her way through the crowd milling about in the hall on 3-West.

"It's a *nurse*," someone cried. "Stop her. Ask her . . ."

A hand shot out and grabbed the white sleeve. "Nurse, do you know—"

"Let go of me, sir, please," the nurse said, pulling away. "What's going on here, anyway?"

"Storm Ryder," a boy in a dirty football uniform said to the nurse. "We're trying to find out about Storm Ryder. Do you know where he is, what happened to him, what's going—"

"No, I don't, I'm sorry," the nurse said, continuing to push through the mob. "I don't know anything about a Mr. Ryder—Ask at the desk who his doctor is—"

"Where's Will, has anyone seen Will?" someone else asked.

"He rode in the ambulance. Where's the coach?"

"I don't know, I thought I saw him—"

"Just a minute!" The voice was sharp and its ring of authority brought instant silence to the large group, who nonetheless jostled and pushed each other to get a look at The Person In Charge.

"I'm Dr. Proctor. I'm a neurologist and one of the doctors on Storm's case."

"Ohhh," the crowd said. "Ahhh."

"Can you tell us anything, Dr. Proctor?" Bonnie squealed.

"We're all his friends, Doc," Rick said. He had forgotten Polly Pratt back at the football field.

"He's a lucky boy to have all these caring friends," Dr. Proctor said. "And he's going to need all of you. I have no information at this time. Now, I'm sorry, but this floor is terribly crowded with you all up here. Could some of you wait downstairs or go home and wait for word? Perhaps if you chose a representative to inform—"

"It's *Sue!*" Matt Argus called. He had arrived with the Roger Gurneys Junior and Senior, who had been covering the game with him for their respective newspapers. "Look, there's Sue!"

The mob made a collective dive for Sue, who had appeared in the corridor.

"Wait, don't maul her!" someone cried.

"Sue! Sue, it's me, Arlette! What's going *on*? I don't know what's going *on!*"

Sue looked at the horde of people facing her and closed her eyes for a moment.

"Sue!" Roger Jr. called. "Tell us about Storm!"

"I can't tell you anything," Sue said softly. They had to strain to hear her. "They won't let me past the door any more, they're working on him . . . His father's there with him . . ."

"Why did he wheel out on the field like that?" Matt called. "Can you tell us what happened?"

"I think he forgot he wasn't playing," Sue said.

"What?" Bonnie said.

"What?" Rick said.

"He what?" Roger Gurney Sr. said.

Sue whispered, "He just forgot he wasn't playing."

*

Nick looked up from his bar-polishing as Mr. Coffee rushed in and slid onto a stool.

"Hey, Mr. Coffee!" he cried. "We've been trying like crazy to reach you. It's about—"

"Just pour me a scotch, Nick. Something really terrible just happened at the game . . ."

"Rackmill won?"

"No, worse. Storm Ryder wheeled out on the field and was tackled."

"*What?*"

"An ambulance took him away. Half the crowd went with him to the hospital. I thought I'd go down later, when there's some news. Give me the drink, Nick. I've never seen anything like it—"

"Do his parents know?" Nick asked.

"I—I guess I just assumed they were in the stands. I'm not sure."

Nick picked up the phone next to the bar. "Bunny wasn't there. She went to the beauty parlor—" He dialed his home number. "Paige?" he said when she answered. "There was an accident at the game. Storm was hurt. See if Bunny knows, if you can get her over to the hospital—" he paused while Paige shot questions at him. "I have no idea, honey, no one knows yet, it just happened. Listen, hang up now and go get Bunny, will you? And get over to the hospital. I'm sure Sue's there, too . . . Yeah . . . Yeah . . . And call me if there's any news. Bye."

He hung up and turned back to Joe Coffee.

"Paige'll take care of it," he said. "But listen, Mr. Coffee, I have a couple of things to say to you—"

"They're publishing my book, Nick," Joe said and raised his glass.

"Well, yeah, that's one of the things—"

"Tacky Press is going to do it. It's not exactly your class publishing company, but they seem to sell an awful lot of—"

"It's what the book's *about,* that's what bothers us, Mr. Coffee. Paige is real upset and so is Sue. You used a lot of stuff from their own lives, Mr. Coffee—"

"It's *fiction,* Nick! I admit I got some ideas from some of the things I've seen and heard, but I made the story up!"

"Well, but *I* may know that and *Paige* may know that and *Sue* may know that and *you* may know that, but is anyone *else* going to know that, Mr. Coffee, that's what I want to know!"

"It's just a *story,* Nick, just a *story!*" Joe insisted.

Nick sighed. "I can't argue with you," he said. "Paige will have to do that. She wants to see you in the worst way about it. But, Mr. Coffee, there's something else you should know. It's real important—"

"Aw, Nick, I can't take any more now . . ."

"This is something you're going to have to take—It's about your—Uh oh . . ." Nick stopped as the door opened.

"What is it?" Joe Coffee asked.

"That guy who just came in," Nick whispered over the bar. "And his friend. They're part of that rowdy crowd."

"You mean that rowdy crowd who's been coming into the bar at night lately?"

"Yeah. Only it's still daytime now and there are two of 'em right there . . ."

Joe half turned on his stool to look and then swung back to face Nick. "Do you think they'll do something?" he asked. "What do you think they'll do?"

"I don't know," Nick said warily, "but I don't like it."

The door opened again and Nick held his breath, but it was Mooch Deener, who smiled and sat down at the bar at the same time the two tough-looking men did.

"I'm on early tonight, Nick, but I've got some time . . . Let's have a—"

"Two beers," one of the two other men said. "Now!"

"Me, too," Mooch said and noticed Joe Coffee. "Joe! I didn't see you!"

"Hi, Mooch—"

"Listen, Joe, have you seen—"

But Nick gave a loud yell. "Hey! What are you doing? What are you doing to my *bar*?"

Mooch Deener and Joe Coffee stared as Nick bent over the bar.

"You—You're *carving* in it!"

"Yeah," the man said with a slow smile. "I never got to finish my name last time."

"You carved—a 'Q' in my bar!" Nick screamed.

"Yeah, I did. And now I got to put in the rest of it so you don't forget me."

"I won't forget you," Nick said as three more men came through the door. He took a deep breath. "Here comes more of 'em," he said, and then turned toward the back room. "Larchmont!" he called. "Hey, Larchmont! Wake up and come on out here! Quick!"

*

The crowd in 3-West's waiting room had thinned. It was almost dinnertime and there was only a small group left. Paige had brought Bunny Ryder to the hospital and was now sitting on a long wooden bench with Sue's head cradled in her lap. Matt Argus was pacing the room clockwise while Arlette paced counterclockwise. The football coach was off in a corner with Roger Gurney Sr. The Ryders were still in another room.

Sue coughed, moaned, rubbed her eyes and sat up. Paige brushed back her niece's hair tenderly. "Are you all right?" she asked.

Sue said, "Uh huh . . ." and then: "Storm?"

"Nothing. Nothing yet, dear."

"Oh."

Roger Sr. broke away from the coach and approached Paige and Sue.

"You're awake," he said softly to Sue.

"Roger," Paige said coldly.

"We meet again," Roger said, evenly. "But I haven't met your niece yet." He held out his hand. "I'm Roger Jr.'s father," he said to Sue.

Sue winced at his grip. "Hello . . . I'm Sue Sudley," she said.

"Yes, my dear, I'd know you anywhere. Frances Faye's little girl."

Paige stood up abruptly. "Listen," she said, ignoring Roger as she smoothed her skirt and faced Sue, "I'm going down to the taproom and get us all something to eat. Something good. Okay?"

"No, Aunt Paige," Sue said with pleading eyes. "I'm not hungry, please don't go . . . Stay here with me . . ."

"I'll go, Mrs. Stillwater," Rick said suddenly, coming

over to them. "You stay here. It's okay. I'll be glad to have something to do."

"Are you sure you don't mind, Rick? That's awfully kind of you," Paige told him.

"Not a bit. Back in a flash. No prob!"

Roger Sr. drifted off as Arlette bounced over.

"That was nice," she said, nodding toward the elevator doors closing behind Rick. "I wonder if he'll bring anything for me. I'll bet not . . ."

"Of course he will," Paige said. "He's getting something for all of us. I told him."

"Was Mr. Coffee here?" Arlette asked. "I looked all over for him."

"I don't know . . ." Sue said, and Paige said, "Hmph" at the mention of the teacher's name.

"I wonder if he's seen his wife yet," Arlette said excitedly.

Sue shook her head and shrugged listlessly.

"Bet he hasn't. Bet he hasn't seen her. I thought I saw her wandering away during halftime. And then things got so, well . . . you know, hectic. Anyway, I can't wait till he runs into her! Is he going to publish that book of his?"

"Sh! Arlette!" Paige said, looking around.

Arlette flopped down on the bench, leaned back and folded her arms. "There's so much to keep track of," she muttered.

"I wish they'd tell us something," Sue said, peering down the corridor. "He's got to be all right, he's just got to be. I simply couldn't stand another—"

"Has anyone seen Dinah today?" Arlette interrupted. "I didn't. I'm sure she wasn't at the game or she would've been here."

"No," Sue sighed, "I didn't see her . . ."

"Hmmm," Arlette said.

A door down the hall opened and the Ryders came out together, Will with his arm tightly around Bunny.

"Oh, they look just *ghastly*," Arlette whispered.

Sue jumped up and ran to meet them. They looked at her with haunted eyes.

"The doctor said 'pretty soon,' Sue," Will Ryder said. "They should know something 'pretty soon' . . ."

*

"See, Mrs. Coffee?" Dinah was saying to a blank Joanna. "This is your apartment building. 427 Richman Road. Remember?" She took Joanna's arm. "Does it ring a bell, Mrs. Coffee? Think now, this is your place. Yours. Mrs. Coffee?"

Joanna said, "Uh . . ."

"Why don't we go inside?" Dinah suggested. She had no idea which apartment the Coffees had shared but she hoped that once inside Mrs. Coffee might automatically steer them to the right one.

Dinah opened the lobby door.

"Here we are, Mrs. Coffee," she said cheerfully. "Where to now?"

Joanna looked around.

"There's the elevator," Dinah said. "Should we get on? What floor?"

Still hopeful, she pressed the elevator button.

"Let's go, Mrs. Coffee," she said as the doors opened. They stepped inside.

"O-kay," Dinah said. "Press your floor button."

Joanna stood there, staring at the closed doors.

"Push your floor button, Mrs. Coffee."

Suddenly the doors opened again and a man got on, carrying a Chihuahua. He glanced at Dinah and Joanna and then pressed the fourth floor button.

"Excuse me, sir," Dinah said, stepping forward. "Do you know this lady? Uh, she lives in this building—"

The Chihuahua turned its little face toward Dinah and growled. Dinah stepped back.

The elevator stopped at the fourth floor and the man got out. Joanna just stood there. Dinah sighed.

"This isn't working, Mrs. Coffee," she said. "Guess we'd better go." She pressed the "lobby" button and tapped her foot restlessly as the elevator descended.

Dinah held the outside glass door open for Joanna and just as she was about to let it go, a white streak raced by her, brushing her leg. Dinah screamed.

"What?" Joanna said.

"I—I don't *know* what it was—" Dinah said and suddenly a small figure crashed into her, nearly knocking her down. "Hey! What's going *on?*" Dinah cried, grabbing the shoulders of the offending child.

"Gee, I'm sorry, I—Hey, is that you, Dinah? I'm Carson. Carson Stillwater. 'Member me? My parents know your parents—"

"I remember you," Dinah said. "Watch where you're going, Carson . . ."

"We were chasing my duck," Carson said, panting. "I'm sorry I banged into you . . ."

"Your *duck?*"

"Yeah. My duck, Marcia. Charlie's getting her. See? There goes Charlie. Don't mind him when you meet him, he's going to say it's *his* duck."

"What are you doing so far from your house, Carson?" Dinah asked. "Are you lost or something?"

"Naw, I'm visiting Marcia. My mom brought me over. See, Marcia's on a vacation at Charlie's house for a while."

Dinah took Joanna's arm and pulled her over to Carson. "Mrs. Coffee, do you remember Carson Stillwater? Do you remember her father—uh—"

"Nick," Carson prompted.

"Nick, right."

Nothing from Joanna.

"My mother is Paige," Carson said helpfully.

Dinah looked from Carson to Joanna.

"And my cousin's name is Sue and my teacher's name is Mrs. Robbins and my Granny Stillwater's name is Marjorie, she lives in Florida now, but she didn't always, only when the weather started bothering her arthritis—"

"Thanks, Carson," Dinah said.

"You're welcome!" Carson said, skipping away. "Anything else you wanna know about me just ask!"

Dinah took a deep breath. "Let's try the bus garage, Mrs. Coffee. You were supposed to drive Storm's special bus this year. Maybe that'll bring it all back to you . . ."

The bus garage was no help. Dinah dragged Joanna from bus to bus, even putting her behind the wheel. Joanna was cooperative but a total blank during all her little tests.

Dinah looked at her and shook her head slowly. "I just don't know what to do with you, Mrs. Coffee," she said, "or where else to take you. I guess we'd just better go to the hospital."

*

The elevator doors burst open.

"Watch the gurney, watch the gurney!" an orderly cried.

"Right here!" Roger Sr. called, hurrying over until he realized they meant the one with wheels.

The man on the gurney moaned softly.

"Oooooh, he's bleeding," Arlette squealed. "How awful!"

"What happened?" Paige asked a nurse who was following.

"It's Larchmont!" Sue screamed. "It's Larchmont on the gurney! His head is bleeding!"

"*What?*" Paige cried and grabbed the nurse's arm. "You've got to tell me what happened!"

The nurse sighed and pulled her arm away. "Just a bar fight," she said. "Some stupid bar fight. The rest of them are down in Emergency."

"Oh, no!" Paige gasped.

"Is Larchmont all right?" Sue asked, grabbing the nurse's other arm. "Is he?"

"Please, please," the nurse said, rubbing her arms. "He'll be all right, he's up here because he was knocked unconscious by a bottle. But it's not serious . . ."

"I'm going down to Emergency," Paige said, hurrying over to the elevator. "I'm sure Nick is there—"

Sue began to bite on her knuckle. "Oh, I don't know what to do . . . Should I go with you, should I stay here, should I—" But as she saw a distraught Paige bump directly into the opening elevator doors, she rushed after her.

"Wait for me!" Arlette cried.

*

"Paigey, the bar's a mess," Nick sighed and then winced as a doctor took another stitch in the side of his hand.

"Never mind that," Paige said. "Are you sure you're all right?"

"I told you I am," he answered. "It's just this cut and these bruises on my arms. Larchmont got it the worst, but they say it's superficial."

"You shoulda seen Rick, Paige," Mooch Deener said. A nurse was putting a large bandage above his eye. "I never saw anyone move so fast."

Rick was lying on the next bed. His arm was in a sling and there was a white slab of plaster over his nose. He was grinning.

"Wasn't anything," he said. "When I walked in, they had it all under control."

"No we didn't," Mooch contradicted. "It was Rick, he really saved the day. This guy they called Nails was about to conk me one with a beer bottle while his buddy was holding me and Rick here takes one look and sails in on 'em with all his strength! And you should've seen what he did to Quigley after he finished Nails off—"

"*Quigley?*" Paige asked.

"Chauncey Quigley. It all started when he carved his name into the bar."

"Just the 'Q' and the 'U'," Nick said. "He only got the 'QU'."

"Well, with a name like that, I guess you can get pretty rowdy," Paige said.

"Rick mashed his nose in his 'Q'," Mooch went on. "And then this guy they called 'The Gouger,' he was about to smash Joe Coffee into the cigarette machine, but Rick—"

"Joe Coffee?" Paige said, arching her eyebrows.

"Hello, Paige," the teacher said, coming up behind her. He was holding an ice pack up to the side of his face. "I came out the best of all of them . . . I brought them down here in my car. Hello there, Sue—"

"Don't you even speak to her," Paige said angrily. "Or to me. You have some nerve, Joe Coffee, acting so friendly and nice after what you've done—"

"Paige, believe me, I never intended to hurt you!" He took the ice pack away from his cheek, revealing a jaw the size and color of an eggplant.

"Oooooh," Arlette murmured.

"I didn't, Paige," the teacher went on as Paige turned her back. "Really, I'd never—"

"Don't be sore at him, Paige," Mooch broke in. "He helped out getting rid of that gang. But Rick really deserves all the credit. You're okay after all, Rick!"

"I didn't do it alone, Mr. Deener. You were pretty good yourself. And Mr. Stillwater and Larchmont. And look at the rowdy crowd over there. They're a lot worse'n we are!" He nodded toward the five men who were crowded into the farthest corner of the Emergency Room. Two of them had been sedated and were sleeping. The others were moaning. "See?" Rick said, grinning.

"I'm not through with you, Joe Coffee," Paige muttered. "You can't imagine what publishing that book could do to our family!"

"Oh, Paige—I really had no idea—"

But suddenly, the electronic doors slid open and in walked Dinah with Joanna Coffee.

"Oh, Rick!" Dinah cried at the sight of his face and arm.

"Dinah!" Mooch yelled.

"Daddy!"

"Joanna!" Joe Coffee gasped.

"Hm?"

*

Following the stitching, the patching and plastering, the bandaging and the ice-packing, everyone moved up to 3-West for word on Storm and Larchmont.

Only Paige, Sue and Nick were allowed in to see the chauffeur who was drifting in and out of consciousness.

"He's a bit foggy now, but he'll be fine tomorrow and you can take him home," the nurse told them. "The X-rays were A-OK."

"Oh, Larchmont," Sue said, her tears falling gently on his hand. "What have we gotten you into?"

"Fine, Miss Sue," he mumbled. "Feel fine . . ."

"You were great, Larch!" Nick said heartily.

"I was great," Larchmont mumbled.

"Sleep now, Larchmont," Sue said, "we'll be back to-morrow."

"Mumble," Larchmont said.

"What, Larchmont? What did you say?" Sue bent over and put her ear next to his lips. "Oh," she said, drawing back.

"What did he say, Sue?" Paige asked.

"He said, 'Nanny'," Sue answered.

*

Joe Coffee's voice was the one Sue heard as she re-entered the waiting room. Someone said, "Sh!" as he was crying, ". . . but she doesn't *know* me! She doesn't *know* me!"

"You mean you came only because of Mrs. Coffee?" Arlette asked Dinah. "You didn't know about Storm?"

"Joanna!" Joe was saying loudly. "Joanna! It's me, *Joe!*"

"She's not *deaf*," a nurse said to him. "She just doesn't *remember.*"

"Of course I didn't know about Storm, how could I, Arlette?" Dinah said. "I wasn't at the game and then I was dragging poor Mrs. Coffee all over town . . ."

"Look, Joanna, look at me! It's Joe, Joanna. *Joe!* Your *husband!*"

"Is Storm going to be okay?" Dinah asked.

Arlette made a face. "Nobody knows yet," she answered.

"Honey," Mooch said, patting Dinah's arm, "that Rick of yours is okay! I was wrong about him, Dinah. You can see him anytime!" And he beamed at Rick, who beamed back.

"Oh, really?" Dinah said.

"Dr. Proctor!" Sue cried. "Look, Dr. Proctor's just come out of Storm's room!"

The Ryders stood up together.

Sue tensed and stared at the doctor.

Everyone stopped talking.

"It's going to be all right," Dr. Proctor said. He was smiling faintly. "He's recovered consciousness and—"

"And what?" Will Ryder said, almost whispering.

"And *what?*" Bunny said anxiously.

"And his left foot—*twitched.*"

*

Paige sighed. "You're right, Nick," she said, looking around at the taproom. "It certainly is a mess!"

"I know. It'll look worse tomorrow in the daylight too . . ."

Paige touched Sue's shoulder. "Honey, I hope you don't mind stopping here on the way home. I just had to see for myself . . ."

"I don't mind at all, Aunt Paige," Sue said. "I don't even feel tired. I'm too numb . . ." She bent over and picked up a broken plant from the floor. Its plastic leaves were covered with something sticky. "Yecch," she said. "Look at this stuff . . ."

"But we're rid of that rowdy crowd," Nick smiled. "They won't be back. I'm sure of it."

"Oh, Nick!" Paige cried. "Look at our beautiful bar! Oh, what a shame, Nick . . ."

"Yeah," he said, shaking his head. "But it only got gouged at one end. See, Paige? It's only over here, these bad gashes. The rest of it's just spilled booze . . ."

"I see . . . only on this end here . . ."

"Well, if it's only on one end, then I've got a terrific idea," Sue said.

"What?"

"I always thought the propeller would look good on the bar. And now that it's bronzed . . . Well, I think I'm ready to let it go—and it would cover up those gashes and look very sporting, Uncle Nick!"

"Very sporting," Nick repeated. "Great idea, Sue! Maybe I'll use a new theme around the place—sports!"

— ✳ —

Two weeks later . . .

Storm sat up in bed and made a face every time Sue stuck the fork in his mouth.

"I can really feed myself, Sue," he said.

"I know, but I want to do something for you, Storm," she told him. "I felt so helpless when we all didn't know what was going to happen to you."

"I still can't get over that we won the game," he said, shaking his head.

"You really won it, you know. The Rackmill boy you tried to tackle was apparently in such a daze after you left, he fumbled a silly pass even before he got hit and our defensive halfback grabbed the ball and ran right into the end zone with it. So you see, it was all because of you that we got that last touchdown, Storm."

"Motrim . . ." Storm mumbled.

"Motrim! Yes, that's what you said in the ambulance, Storm! You told it in the ambulance, just the way it happened!"

"I had a dream . . ." Storm said.

"I wonder if you got some special powers as a result of the accident, Storm," Sue said thoughtfully.

"You didn't see it, Sue? The rest of the game?"

"Of course I didn't see it! Did you think I'd stay at the game after you were hit? We all heard about it afterwards."

"Sorry I scared you all so badly," Storm said. He opened his mouth and Sue shoveled in a mound of mashed potatoes.

"I think it was worth it, Storm . . . What you went through, what all of us went through," Sue said.

"You mean because—"

"Now don't talk with your mouth full," Sue said and filled it again. "Yes, I mean because of the freakiness of your accident your legs are going to heal!"

＊

Sue tiptoed out of Storm's room when she was sure he was asleep.

Dinah was sitting on the couch in the waiting room, writing furiously, her tongue sticking out of a corner of her mouth.

"Hi, Dinah," Sue said. "Almost finished?"

"Hi, Sue. Storm okay?"

"He's sleeping. How's your story coming?"

"I'm nearly through," Dinah said proudly. "Six pages! Can you believe it? I never wrote so much in my life! 'The Video Games Habit and How I Kicked It,' by Dinah Deener. And all grammatically correct, too!" She held up the papers proudly.

Sue sat down next to her. "I'm really proud of you, Dinah. Your parents must be proud, too. Look at all you've done in just two weeks. You're going to do so well on your English midterms!"

"I know, and it's all because of you, Sue. I'm glad you won our bet. Now that I'm clean, the thought of a whole weekend at Leon's Neon makes me sick to my stomach . . ."

"Rick must be proud of you, too," Sue said.

"Oh . . . Rick . . . yeah . . . You know, my father really likes him now. He keeps inviting him over. Rick's around my house all the time."

"Oh, that must make you happy," Sue said.

Dinah chewed the end of her pencil. "Mmmm," she said absently. "You'd think so, wouldn't you?"

*

Nick took his can of Pledge and put it away on a shelf under the bar. Then he reached for his bottle of Wesson oil, dabbed a little on an old diaper of Carson's, and lovingly began to rub it over the blades of the bronzed propeller. He was smiling to himself when Joe Coffee sat down and ordered a light beer.

"No more scotch, Mr. Coffee?" Nick asked.

"Nah, I need my wits about me at all times, Nick," Joe said. "Joanna needs me. Say . . . propeller looks nice."

"I can see my face in the blades," Nick grinned. "Nice decoration, huh? Goes with the fish."

"Covers up the scratched bar, too," Joe Coffee said. "The place looks good as new."

"Sure does. The whole football team came in and cleaned up for me. Great bunch of guys. Paige cried. By the way, how's Joanna doing?"

"Joanna? She's great. Doesn't remember me or our marriage at all, but funny—she just fell in love with me at first sight! The girl's crazy about me!"

"I'm happy for you, Mr. Coffee," Nick said. "But it wasn't first sight, really . . ."

"For her it was. It's like a brand new romance. I feel just like a kid again!"

Nick smiled. "Well, I guess that's one of the reasons you don't mind. About your book, I mean."

"Well, Nick . . . When I realized how much it would hurt Sue and Paige . . . I just couldn't go through with it. I didn't sign with Tacky Press after all. What I'm going to do, though, is try to revise it."

"How?"

"Well, I thought I'd visit some neighboring towns . . . sit in some bars and restaurants . . . listen to people. Maybe get a few new ideas."

Nick nodded.

"Yes," the teacher went on, "that's what I think I'll do. Listening to people is a wonderful way to find characters and plots . . ."

"But not so close to home," Nick warned.

"Oh, yes, right . . . But I'm going to need a lot of new ideas . . . and fast, too. Hmmmm . . . ."

"What is it, Mr. Coffee?"

"I was just thinking . . . Maybe I'll take Arlette with me."

*

Mooch Deener bit into his lox-bacon-and-cheese-on-a-bagel just as the bus from the east pulled in.

"Four," he said to himself and then almost immediately, "no, it's Wednesday. Two. I bet it's two." He chewed slowly and watched. "Yay!" he cried as he saw two shadows emerge and step down to the platform. He licked a paper gold star and pasted it to today's date on his calendar. "Guessed right again," he mumbled happily. "Third day in a row!"

He looked at the two people. A youngish man with

his nose buried in *Variety,* and a little old lady. He made a face as the man let the glass door slam on her.

"Hey!" Mooch called. "Get the door for the little old lady!"

"Yeah, man, okay . . ." He got the door without looking up from his paper.

Something familiar about that guy, Mooch thought, watching him. The little old lady staggered past him, pulling one large suitcase on wheels by a rope in her teeth, and carrying two others in each hand.

The man was wearing dark glasses, a purple T-shirt and chinos, and was carrying a pink-and-turquoise nylon travel bag.

"Leon!" Mooch cried. "Hey, Leon, is that you?"

The man looked up finally. "Uh, yeah, man, how are ya."

"You've come back!" Mooch cried.

"Yeah, man, obviously," Leon said. "Sorry I missed, uh, Homecoming."

"Where did you come from, Leon?" Mooch asked. "I thought you were in Toledo."

"No, man, why'd you think that?"

"Well, because Joanna—er, I mean—Uh, no reason . . ."

"I was in New York, man, the Big Apple."

"New York?"

"New York, yeah, man. That's where it's at. And I'm going back there just as soon as I clear up a little business."

"What business?" Mooch asked.

"See ya around, man," Leon said, and tipped his shades in a salute.

*

"*Nanny!*" Sue cried, leaping toward the little old lady standing in the Stillwaters' doorway. "Nanny! I don't believe it, is it really you?" She hugged her tightly.

Nanny took the rope out of her mouth and put down the other suitcases. "Yes, Miss Sue, it's really your Nanny, all the way from Suddenly! I came just as soon as your aunt called."

"Aunt Paige called? She didn't tell me!"

"No, she wanted to surprise you. Larchmont, too. Where is the old thing!" Nanny blushed.

"Oh, he's back at the bar, Nanny. He stayed here for a while until he was completely recovered . . . I guess Aunt Paige told you . . ."

"She surely did. The old thing! That's why I'm here. And of course, to see you, my little baby!" she added. "My, but you look wonderful! That Suddenly pallor is all gone, and replaced by Palatine pinkness! Just look at those cheeks!" She pinched one of them. "Where's the rest of the family, Miss Sue?"

"Well, Uncle Nick's down at the bar and Aunt Paige took Carson over to visit Charlie Hegelmeyer and his duck. Why don't I just take you upstairs to the guest room so you can lie down after your exhausting trip?"

"I'm not exhausted, dear," Nanny said. "I'd like to go right over and see Larchmont and surprise him. The old thing! Would that be all right?"

"Nanny, are you sure you're up to it? Pulling that suitcase all the way here by your teeth . . ."

"Let's go, Miss Sue!" Nanny cried and smacked her fist into her palm.

*

Charlie Hegelmeyer played with a blade of grass while Carson continued to force-feed the duck.

"He won't eat that way, Carson," Charlie sighed. "I keep telling you."

"It's a *she*, Charlie, and she *always* ate this way when I had her. She likes it. Don't you, Marcia?"

Charlie went back to his blade of grass. He didn't bother to contradict her. The truth was, he'd been calling the duck 'Marcia' himself, since Carson had been coming to visit. It seemed to fit, especially since Carson had tied a lacy pink bow around the duck's neck.

"Carson, let's do something else now. I'm tired of playing with the duck," Charlie said.

"Well . . ."

"Come on, Carson."

She patted the duck, walked over and sat down next to Charlie. "What do you want to play?" she asked.

"Well . . ." Charlie said with a sly grin, "I got a *collection*. It's buried behind the garage, so I can dig it up when I want and my mother can't watch me from the kitchen window. We could go dig it up now and you can see it."

"What is it?" Carson asked.

"I told you. It's my *collection*."

"But a collection has to be *of* something, Charlie. What's it *of*?"

"What's *what* of?"

"Your collection! The one you buried behind the garage!" Carson screamed with her hands on her hips.

"What about it?" Charlie asked.

Carson frowned at Charlie, then relaxed her stance. "I forget," she said. "Let's go dig it up."

Fifteen minutes later, Mrs. Hegelmeyer yelled from the back door: "Charlie! Carson! Where are you?"

In a minute they appeared at the side of the garage.

"What were you two doing?" Mrs. Hegelmeyer asked.

"Playin'," Charlie answered with a shrug.

"Well, where's your duck, young man?"

Charlie sucked in his breath.

"Oh my gosh, Marcia's gone!" Carson gasped and began to cry.

"Gee-ee-e," Charlie wailed. "We just left him for a minute . . ."

"Charlie, you're so *dumb!*" Carson shrieked.

*

Larchmont, standing next to a blade of the propeller at the end of the bar, was the first to see Nanny and Sue come through the door and he gripped a stool as his heart leaped.

"Nanny . . ." he whispered. "Nanny Grossup!"

"You old thing!" she cried, running to hug him as he blushed furiously.

"But what—"

"Miss Sue's Aunt Paige called me. Told me everything. Just couldn't stay away!"

"But the Senior Citizens' summer camp—?"

"Yes, they're calling it The Twilight Zone. Isn't that cute? Well, they'll just have to do without me. I wanted to be with you. I missed you, you old thing!"

"Oh," Larchmont said and hugged her back. "Oh," he said again. "It's just so lovely to see you . . ."

Sue beamed at them from across the room.

"Pretty mushy stuff, there, old folks," a man at the bar said, looking up from his *Variety.*

Nanny and Larchmont glared at him.

Leon removed his shades and smiled. Then he drew in his breath and dropped his jaw as he got a good look at Nanny.

"Mother!" he cried.

— * —

A few scenes
from our next episode . . .

Roger Gurney Sr. meets Paige at the library. He si-
dles up to her.

"Paige, I've heard about Joe Coffee's book and I know
what's in it."

"Thank heavens he's not publishing it, Roger Gurney,
so you just forget it. Even though he made it all up, I
wouldn't want a single soul to think it has a chance of
being true! How did you find out about it, anyway?"

"Well, Paige, you can't negate a notorious nose for
news, now, can you? I didn't get to be the publisher of
the *Palatine P.M.-Daily* for nothing, did I? And as for
Joe's book being fiction, well, I wouldn't negate that
either, Paige."

"Don't you try—"

Roger faces her. "I made a trip to New York shortly
after Frances Faye left town, Paige."

"You did not, Roger. You went to Findlay to visit
your cousin."

"No, Paige, New York."

"Not Findlay?"

"New York."

"But Roger, your wife was alive then! You were married then!"

"Think back, Paige. I wasn't married to Miriam then."

"Roger, you don't mean . . ."

"Yes."

"*Sue?*"

"Frances Faye and I were together in New York, Paige. I wasn't going to let you and your family come between us any more."

"We never tried to come between you, Roger. That's why I don't believe you. Frances Faye ran away on her own. You'd say anything to bring her back—to you, to life—but it won't work, Roger Gurney!"

"I *do* want her back, Paige! I *do!*"

*

Rick is on his knees.

"Dinah, won't you go out with me tonight?" he pleads.

"Sorry, Rick, I'm busy. I've got a date."

"A date? Who with? I'll kill him, Dinah!"

Dinah sighs. "Roger Gurney Jr., that's who, Rick. And don't you dare touch him. He's got more smarts in his little finger than you'll ever have, and we're going to be co-editors of *The Palatine Prattler!* You can go visit my father. He'll be thrilled!"

*

Nanny and Larchmont, their arms around each other's waists, face Leon at his desk in the Leon's Neon office.

"But Leon," Nanny entreats, "where have you *been* for nineteen years?"

Leon leans back in his swivel chair. "Oh, around, Ma . . . You know, when you got that job at Suddenly and put me in that foster home, I just figured it was time to cut out on my own."

Nanny wrings her hands. "But Leon, I planned to bring you to Suddenly to be with me! Just as soon as I explained to the Sudleys I had a fourteen-year-old son . . ."

"Don't worry about it, Ma," Leon says with a cavalier wave. "I made out okay. Now you and Larchmont, here—well, I don't know what you cute old folks have in mind, but I came back here to sell Leon's Neon and go into show business, and I'm real glad you two are buying the place . . . What are you going to do with it, anyway?"

Larchmont grips Nanny's waist tighter. "Well, Leon, we were thinking of turning it into a tearoom . . ."

*

Matt Argus tiptoes into the supply room. He looks around to make absolutely sure no one is watching.

"The answer keys to the midterms are around here somewhere," he mutters to himself. "That's where they were last year . . ." He takes down a large box labeled *Typing Paper*. "Betcha Mr. Coffee hid them in here," Matt mumbles. "Last time they were in a carbon paper box . . . took me three days to find 'em . . ."

Matt opens the box and frowns.

"*This Time of Passion?*" Matt reads out loud. "Now what the heck is *this?*"

*

Storm and Sue, in sweatshirts and shorts, are jogging around the Palatine reservoir. Sue is panting.

"Storm! Slow down! I just can't keep up with you!"

"Okay, Sue, okay," Storm says. "I'm just getting my jogging pace back . . . Hey, Knuckles! Here, boy!"

The dog trots over to them happily and Sue pets him.

"He certainly has changed, Storm," she says.

"No, he was always like this before I got hurt. Hey, where's he going?"

They watch the dog, seemingly on the trail of something, head for some nearby bushes.

"He probably saw a squirrel," Sue says. "Oh, Storm, the way you're going, the progress you're making . . . I just know you'll be back on the football squad next fall!"

Storm sways slightly. He stares out at the calm waters of the reservoir. "I *will* be back on the squad . . . I will . . ." His eyes glaze. Suddenly, he cries out: "It's Ryder! He's going all the way! No one can touch him! The first Palatine goal of the year, and it's all Number Forty Four's—Storm Ryder!"

"Storm?" Sue says hesitantly.

"Huh?"

"What did you say about scoring the first goal of the season?"

Storm shrugs. "I dunno, what'd I say?"

"Nothing, I guess . . ." Sue says, frowning.

"Sue, will you be in the stands cheering for me if— *when* I get back on the squad again?"

"Of course, Storm . . . Of course, I will. Are you ready to run again or are you feeling tired?"

"I'm not tired at all! Where's Knuckles?"

They see the dog digging frantically in the bushes with his front paws.

"Knuckles!" Storm cries. "Come here, boy!"

The dog whines, but comes over to Storm. Sue notices a white feather in his mouth. She races over to the bushes and parts them.

"Oh, Storm!" she cries. "Will you look at this!"

"What is it?" He walks over and sees for himself.

"A duck with a ribbon," he says with a grin.

"Sitting on a nest," Sue says, smiling with him. "Carson was right. It's a female."

"Funny place for a nest," Storm muses.

"Well, Marcia's a funny duck," Sue says. "I think we'll let her be. What do you think?"

Storm, still grinning, nods and they begin to jog again.

"Sue," he says as they run, "you and my being able to walk again are just about the best things that ever happened to me in my life."

"That's a lovely thing to say, Storm," Sue says. She jogs harder in order to keep up with him. They wave at Bonnie Finster, who whizzes by on a bicycle. Sue's fingers touch Storm's arm. "You know," she says, "I came to Palatine to be a real teenager. To learn to live a perfectly normal life and be just like all the other kids. Storm?"

"What, Sue?"

"Is this it?"

— ✳ —

Also by Judie Angell

Dear Lola
or How to Build Your Own Family

A Word from Our Sponsor
or My Friend Alfred

The Buffalo Nickel Blues Band

In Summertime It's Tuffy

Tina Gogo

What's Best for You

Ronnie and Rosey

Secret Selves

28 DAYS

DATE DUE			
DEC 16 2001			

Juvenile FICTION
Angell, Judie.
Suds, a new daytime drama